THE IMMORTALITY WARS

THE
PENITENT

PART I

A. KEITH CARREIRO

2 November 2019

COPPER
BEECH
PRESS

First Stillwater River Publications Edition 2019.

ISBN-10: 1-950339-28-9
ISBN-13: 978-1-950339-28-0

1 2 3 4 5 6 7 8 9 10
Written by A. Keith Carreiro.
Cover art by Hollis Michaela. www.hollismichaela.com
Published by Stillwater River Publications, Pawtucket, RI, USA.

Publisher's Cataloging-In-Publication Data
(Prepared by The Donohue Group, Inc.)

Names: Carreiro, A. Keith, author.
Title: The Penitent. Part I / A. Keith Carreiro.
Description: First Stillwater River Publications edition. | Pawtucket, RI, USA : Stillwater
    River Publications, 2019. | Series: The immortality wars
Identifiers: ISBN 9781950339280 | ISBN 1950339289
Subjects: LCSH: Soldiers--Fiction. | Good and evil--Fiction. | Faith--Fiction. | Self-
    realization--Fiction. | Speculative fiction. | GSAFD: Christian fiction. | LCGFT:
    Allegories. | Fantasy fiction.
Classification: LCC PS3603.A774375 P46 2019 | DDC 813/.6--dc23

Connect with Keith on his website
or other social media platforms:

https://immortalitywars.com
https://www.facebook.com/keith.carreiro.33
https://instagram.com/immortalitywars/
https://twitter.com/immortalitywars
https://www.linkedin.com/in/keith-carreiro-5040aa17/
https://www.goodreads.com/author/show/15959901
https://reedsy.com/author/a-keith-carreiro

To the storytellers in our lives...

FOR PAUL,
I HOPE THAT YOU
ENJOY READING THIS
STORY.

BEST

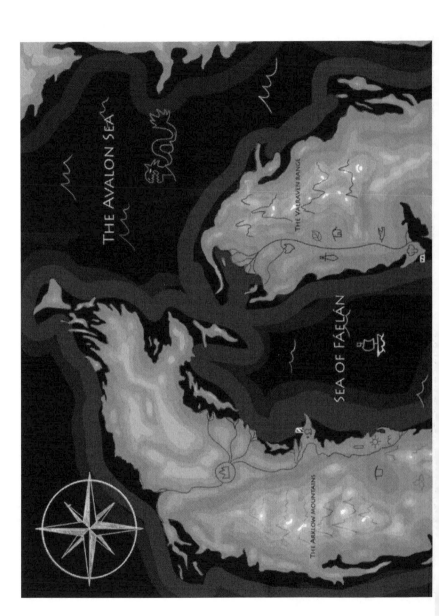

THE WESTERN ISLES

- ⌂ THE REFUGE
- ⌘ THE FEN
- ⌖ ST AYRWYLIS PRIORY
- ✳ DAWNS ABBEY
- ⌒ THE VAIL OF NAOMHIN
- ▯ THE RINGING BAY
- Ω TRABAILE
- ⛰ TERMONDON
- ❘ RIVER WYTHE

WEST FUNDLAND

- ♔ THE CAPITAL
- ⚔ BATTLEFIELD
- ⌂ FARM
- ⌐ GULLSWATER
- ⌘ SEASCALE
- ▧ THE GREAT BAY
- ◩ LIMESTONE QUARRY
- | THE FORGOTTEN RIVER
- ⌖ THE DEMESNE OF
  THE COPPER BEECHES

SEA OF NINIAN

THE DROOM PEAKS

THE BELT OF IRIA

ACKNOWLEDGMENTS

Psalm 51:16-17 is from The Living Bible copyright © 1971. Used by permission of Tyndale House Publishers, Inc., Carol Stream, Illinois 60188. All rights reserved.

Shakespeare, William. "Literature Network – William Shakespeare – King Lear – Act 5. Scene III." *The Literature Network*. Jalic Inc., 2000-2016. Web. 12 Mar. 2016. http://www.online-literature.com /Shake speare/kinglear/27/

Spenser, Edmund. "Edmund Spenser – The Faerie Queene – Canto I." *The Literature Network*. Jalic Inc., 2000-2016. Web. 12 Mar. 2016. http://www.online-literature.com/edmund-spenser/ faerie-queene/2/

A debt of thanks to Dawn and Steven R. Porter, Stillwater River Publications, for their help and expertise in making this print-on-demand novel possible.

Without Hollis Machala's visual expertise, her creative genius, and kind patience with me in helping develop the exterior and interior formatting of *the Penitent*, this story would still be in manuscript form. A deep debt of thanks goes to her for her invaluable assistance in helping make an idea be beautifully visible.

Jamie Forgetta is a freelance illustrator, author, and designer who worked with me for the first six months of 2019. She designed the three maps used in this trilogy. Many thanks to her for her superbly crafted visual work. Her patience is amazing and her ability to collaborate effectively with an author having no visual talent whatsoever is a miracle in itself. The quality of her work speaks for itself. She helped inspire some of the names of streets in the Seascale map and helped in getting some of the mountain ranges named for the main map depicting the setting of *the Penitent*. Her website is www, jamieforgetta.wixsite.com/portfolio

Thanks, also, to my daughter, Chelsea Snyder, for her help in designing the cover, especially at the beginning stages of design.

A deep and abiding thanks goes to Carolyn for her support of this story, and for her helping edit the first draft. The same thanks goes to Kellie Kilgore for her editing help as well.

I have seen the day, with my good biting falchion
I would have made them skip...

— William Shakespeare (1564–1616),
King Lear (1608)
— Act V, Scene iii, ll. 276 & 277

Led with delight, they thus beguile the way,
Vntill the blustering storme is ouerblowne;
When weening to returne, whence they did stray,
They cannot finde that path, which first was showne,
But wander too and fro in ways vnknowne,
Furthest from end then, when they nearest weene,
That makes them doubt, their wits be not their owne:
So many paths, so many turnings seene,
That which of them to take, in diuerse doubt they been.

— Edmund Spenser (1552–1599), *The Faerie Qveene* (1590)
— The First Book of The Faerie Qveene *Contayning*
— The Legende of the Knight of the Red Crosse, *or* of Holinesse
—Canto I, Stanza X

[16] You don't want penance;[a] if you did, how gladly I would do it!
You aren't interested in offerings burned before you on the altar.
[17] It is a broken spirit you want—remorse and penitence. A broken
and contrite heart, O God, you will not ignore.

— Psalm 51:16 & 17 (*The Living Bible*)

Footnotes:
[a]Psalm 51:16 *penance*, literally "a sacrifice"

PROLOGUE | PROPOSITIONS SIX*

The singularity that is inevitably coming will be man and Lucifer's chance to carve out a place; if not yet above, but alongside, the Creator's. Mankind will truly learn what it means to <u>disassemble</u>. The rest of us will be brought into this <u>dystopic</u>[40] montage[41] of evil playing itself out presently on the world canvas in a vast sense of di<u>se</u>ase. It will be a contagion of mind and a pandemic of conscience fluorescing into all levels of humanity's values at greater and exponentially increasing rates. There will be an avalanche of deceit in which people will earnestly embrace as the truth.

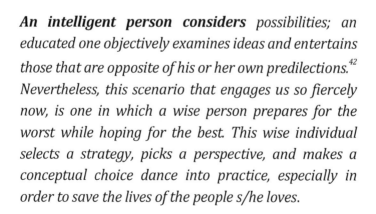

An intelligent person considers possibilities; an educated one objectively examines ideas and entertains those that are opposite of his or her own predilections.[42] Nevertheless, this scenario that engages us so fiercely now, is one in which a wise person prepares for the worst while hoping for the best. This wise individual selects a strategy, picks a perspective, and makes a conceptual choice dance into practice, especially in order to save the lives of the people s/he loves.

If we but listen figuratively to such wisdom, we could at least consider my statement here as a thought experiment—an ideational exercise. Affectively, I am sure that it translates well into a trenchant cry in at least three of the world's three great Abrahamic religions: "Gird your loins with the full armor of God.[246] The angels will trumpet[247] in Armageddon.[248] The seals will be opened.[249] The vials will be poured out[250]: The Four Horsemen[251] will canter forth an Apocalypse[252] unto the world's attention."

These occurrences are ancient in their determination to happen. They are inexorable in their proleptic[156] demand for such reality to blossom into our own time, and their very need to unfold into a preordained, historical manifestation only indicates impatient hesitation on their behalf, as well as the momentum guiding them; yet, they will but presently ensue in full force.

Such causes await their attendant effects; they have to proceed because all the forces and omens[51] are assembling into play for them to ignite into being, into

an outpouring that includes mythology, legend and wisdom equally being awakened. Thus, today I await for the Cumaean sibyl[016] to offer her insight into the future; I anticipate a fifteenth book of the Sibylline Oracles[017] to be newly found and read to mankind; and, I pray that I live to hear the voices of a Daniel and a Matthew, a thaumaturge, a nabi or a Tay al-Ard speak aloud of it to me.

I envy Simeon who in his old *age still tarried on Earth, within the holy temple of ancient Jerusalem, waiting for the consolation of Israel.[14-15]*

-Professor Melvin Tobin, Ph.D.
-Cambridge, Massachusetts, Old Earth

*Statement first excerpted from a retirement speech, "Utopia Imperiled," given by Dr. Tobin at the Harvard Club.

Tobin, M. (2156, July 15). †The philosophical primacy[1] of intelligence engineering[2] permeating throughout advanced evolutionary intervention.56 The Journal of Ideation & Consilience, Hologram Codex 18: 2287.299 | 12 – NASCENT: 2057-2058. Retrieved Epicycle 07, 2252

CHAPTER ONE

He finally found the chance to lie down in the predawn hour. He was tired beyond his capacity to care about putting the threadbare blanket over him. It had been given to him not so long ago in the early morning hours. The night was enough for him. Instead of using the blanket beside him, he wrapped the evening around him darkly. Appropriate for his mood.

He smiled bleakly at the irony between himself and the blanket. *We are two of a kind. Worn out from use. Tired, tattered. Timeworn.*

After a long while of staring at the inside of his eyelids when sleep simply evaded him, he stood up and went to sit between the roots at the base of a large tree. He shrugged himself into a comfortable position against the smooth bark. His mind cast itself back to the beginning of the day before. It was not a good memory.

Even though it had been nine in the morning, the battle already had been over for several hours. Shrugging off two bodies that had collapsed on top of him, he stood up, surveying with great curiosity what was around him. The dead stretched to the end

1

of his sight in all directions. Cries, moans, cursing, and weeping—from those still alive—shared time with the sound of the ravens and crows who took advantage of this tribute of war. They fed greedily on the dead horses and harvest of warriors, battling in their own turn as the mortals and their mounts did earlier with one another, over the choicest of morsels to be found for their ravening palate. Their sing–song clamor had a keening and urgency that matched his own mood. An aftermath of woe, anger, delight and hunger that seemingly could not be filled.

He took a sword–ripped cloak from a fallen officer and wiped the remains of combat off himself. Unknowingly, he took back the two–edged, falchion sword he had wielded in hand–to–hand fighting from the body of the last slain soldier he had killed. The sound of its being withdrawn from the corpse did not sicken him physically as much as it repulsed his sense of order and balance in the world. He wiped off the sword and sheathed the blade in his empty scabbard. Both of his hands searched for knives on his belt that were not present.

At that moment in time, he did not think that taking any living being from the world in such fashion created a balance of harmony in the universe. Not so much that he was a philosopher of such rationality, it was something he felt deeply inside himself. He threw the cloak, now filthy from the gore of war, away without consciously thinking about it.

In his empathy with the crying of the birds around him, each warrior he had felled in his life as a soldier took a toll from him. He could feel each man and youth in battle that he had killed scream in the frustration and fear of their being separated from the thin thread of life. He felt old. Neither the energy of his youth nor the power in the force of his arms gave him confidence. He felt jaded beyond belief. All he wanted to do was to find rest. An oasis of peace to help still the rage filling the world around him.

The sun waged its own war with an oncoming storm. Wind swept by him in fitful gusts. Sunlight seemed shattered by clouds parrying it away from shining down onto the scenes around him. Shadows coursed by, sounding in his mind as harp strings plucked by an angel of war. Like furies in pursuit of vengeance they screamed by him in flickering vibration. Untouched by their ire he sought a nearby stream that he had passed over the night before.

No one approached him because it seemed as though there was no one there able to do so. In his present condition, he was alone with his thoughts to estrange him from his own company.

CHAPTER TWO

It took him a while to leave the killing fields behind him.

The young warrior found it difficult to walk. He saw, soon enough after arising from the battlefield that blood was slowly leaking from a wound to the back of his head. He had to rest often. He stumbled constantly. Fatigue, thirst, a craving to eat, loss of blood and the shock of battle, all took their toll on him. After what seemed like a long time, he discovered that he was going in a large circle on the outside edge of the field of war. He sank to his knees and blacked out onto the ground.

His father was talking to him. The older man's grey eyes looked deeply into the boy's own. He was being told something very solemn.

"You must never forget," he informed him, "that we lost your mother when you were born. I don't blame you for that, but we both now have shared her loss for five years. I'm still a young man. I'm in the pride of my life. I want a wife and more children to raise around me. Are you listening to me, boy?"

"Yes, Da," he responded steadfastly to his father's question.

"Unfathomable as it seems to me, what with everything so ill that happened then, I have found another woman. She is everything I can ask for. She will be moving in with us soon."

The boy frowned at this news. He was puzzled at what his father was telling him. He was not sure that having a new mother was what he wanted. He was used to things being the way he knew them to be.

"Your mother was the light of my life, don't you ever forget that," his father continued. "When she passed, the glow of her shining in my world was snuffed out faster than a candle being put out in a gale. The candle that was her life had all its tallow and beeswax taken completely away. There was nothing else left to make light.

"At least, now, while you and I cannot relight that same candle, we can rekindle another and let its light shine, so that love again fills our lives with its glow."

The shutters and doorway to the street were wide open. The boy could hear the sounds of the village outside. The light of day poured into the room in which his father was talking to him. As he loved his father so much, he tried to understand what his dad was trying to say to him.

A tear formed in one of his father's eyes. It grew large enough to spill down the cheek bone of his face. It dropped on the back of the boy's right hand, which was resting on a table in front of him.

As the tear dropped from his hand onto the boy's hand, his father said, "The night your mother died, God rest her soul, I had a shroud—a linen cloth—placed over her head and the length of her body. When I put it on her, I had to remove you from around her dead arms. You were very quiet for a first–born one. The mid–wife wouldn't touch you. Said you were a bad omen. I was the one who placed you on your mother's stomach just before she died."

His father paused in the telling of his son's birth. He stood upright and looked out the nearby window. Hawkers in the lane were crying out for their wares of cloth, rags, and vegetables to be sold to passersby and to those within doors hearing their sing–song voices spill out the value of their goods.

"I was crushed by this...," his father did not finish his statement. He let the phrase drop away from him. Instead, he cast out his arms to indicate everything around him. He bowed his head.

He looked up again and then at the boy sitting in front of him. "Your mother wanted your name to be Paul. Like her father," he explained. "With that cloth covering over her," he said, "and everything else. With the darkness and gloom of her passing on me and you, I named you Pall—with a double L."

6

The memory of that day passed. He opened his eyes and saw that he was still on the edge of the battlefield. He sat up off the ground and looked at the carnage all around him. The crows and ravens swooped everywhere on the field. They fought one another for the best pieces and morsels of the dead. The darkness of a violent storm rapidly approached.

CHAPTER THREE

He finally knelt down at the edge of the stream he had been seeking. As he scooped a cupped hand of water close to his mouth, he smelled a coppery flavor from it. He let the remaining amount of water fall away to the ground when he saw that it was completely red in his hand. The stream swirled by him gurgling in what sounded like muted death rattles.

"Not much to look at or smell, but once you get it past your nose and eyes, it does what it's supposed to do," said a man standing up across from him on the other side of the creek. He was tall and dressed in the garb of many of the fallen warriors he had seen on the battlefield. His bow, already fully bent, was in his steady hands, nocked with an arrow. It was fletched with two barred green hens and a solid blue vane for the middle feather.

Looking at him from across the stream, the man looked formidable. The arrow was perfection in itself, not crooked as poplar would be no matter the finesse in the craftsmanship of the arrow maker. *Birch, probably. Maybe spruce*, he thought to himself. He also saw that the almost seven-foot length of the bow was comfortably being held with what appeared to be a 36-inch arrow. He became amazed, even tongue-tied, when he saw that the draw length had to be between 160 to 180 pounds.

"Not much of a talker, eh," stated the bowman. "Tell you what; come across the stream over to me. Don't make any sudden moves."

Out of curiosity rather than fear, he did as he was instructed to do. He struggled with his memory upon sight of this giant. He was almost certain that he had met another of his size. *Perhaps the same one*, he thought.

Aspen leaves behind him on the bank shivered in a slight breeze that started as he approached midway in the stream. It was getting noticeably cooler. The sunlight, what had been left of it before, disappeared entirely.

"Stop right there," he was told. "Let's have a little palaver, you and me. That is, if you see fit to join in. Otherwise, ain't much purpose of me just holding this thing drawn at you. May as well just let fly and forget the jawin."

He watched the man's eyes intently. He tried to see how he was breathing. His talking disarmed him even more completely. A slight smile started to form on the young soldier's face.

"Now if I didn't think you were a total fool before, I'm beginning to believe you're daft, what with that half smile you're startin to get goin there now." The man shifted slightly to his right about four feet.

Closer to my heart, he mused silently.

"Either you're going to tell me your name, or I'll just call you Dead," the bowman said to him.

He started walking again toward his adversary. Slowly. It started raining fitfully. "Pall—with a double L," he responded.

Just then, the shoulder of a body floating by in the stream touched him. He looked down at it and frowned. Entangling with him, it stopped his forward progress across the stream.

"Friend of yours? Or enemy?"

He shrugged, not saying anything else aloud.

"Like I said, not too conversational." He beckoned him to approach closer with a slight diagonal jerk of his head.

Pall pushed the floating corpse away from him. Gently. Firmly. With respect, not repugnance. The bowman nodded approval at this gesture, while moving another four feet to the right. The bow remained fully drawn in a rock solid fashion.

The water level was now barely to Pall's knees. The breeze began in earnest to become fitful and more forceful. The rain paused in its downfall toward the two men on the ground. It became noticeably cooler.

"When you reach my side of the bank, take a seat right there." The bowman pointed with his chin to indicate the spot where the young man first saw him stand up in front of him.

The water still blushed vermilion as Pall reached the stream bank. He sat down and as he did so, the bowman moved in front of him, facing the stream while the young man's back was turned away from it.

"John Savage," he said.

The young soldier nodded in turn to this introduction. The breeze changed almost to a gale. Tree limbs, branches, even the younger tree trunks, moved in chaotic thrumming to its sway.

"I take it that you just arrived from that field of killing a mile back, south of here," Savage stated.

Another nod was given in reply to this statement.

The arrow remained trained on his heart. Ten feet away from him.

Lightning flashed.

"Where's the rest of your comrades?"

He shrugged his shoulders and gave a quizzical look at Savage.

A boom of thunder bellowed from what seemed like the bottom of the world.

"Well, silent Pall with a double L, what kind of name is that?"

"It means a shroud that's put over the dead," he replied.

For the first time since Pall originally saw him, Savage shivered.

Lightning struck again. A clap of thunder stuttered into being almost in time with the

11

suddenness of its searing light. The wind stopped. Rain, as if in vengeance of the death that occurred earlier all around them, came down in a merciless torrent.

CHAPTER FOUR

Savage lowered his bow, taking almost all of the tension out of the draw. The arrow remained nocked, though. "Well, ain't this a treat," he said, without specifically indicating whether or not he meant the weather, the situation between them, or the battle that had occurred earlier.

The rain became a downpour.

"Save that thought about the shroud thing," he said in a louder voice in order to be heard over the pouring rain. "There's a farmstead up ahead in the woods that I passed by earlier in the day. Let's get over to it and out of this weather."

The bowman turned around quickly and started running into the forest.

The young man looked bemused at the fast retreating back of the man whom he first thought was an erstwhile opponent. What with the rain, the darkness from the storm and the deepening gloom already beginning at the edge of the woods, he started into a quick trot in order not to lose sight of him.

He moved into the beauty of a sylvan woodland. It was an ancient Weald. Oaks, maples and a brilliant glowing of a stand of birch on his right grew among huge copper beech trees. The sides of their trunks shone soft silver in the remaining light. The deep burgundy to purple color of their leaves shimmered, making everything appear as if it were cast in crimson and amaranth. Because of the thick canopy of trees overhead, the rain barely reached them as they went deeper into the depths of the forest.

In the light cast by these trees, Savage burned ahead into the heart of the wood.

Despite the demands of trying to keep Savage in sight, Pall was trying to look around and absorb the beauty of the place through which he was passing.

I would like to come back and spend more time here, he mused, as his feet sank into the ancient duff and mossy areas of the ground around him.

He thought he heard the brief rattle of thunder and the faint hint of wind far above him.

Without the damage of war on the land, I wonder if I could catch any fish in that stream I just crossed?

Another part of his awareness started wondering about Savage: *Why had he been where I first saw him? Who is he, anyway? Why is he alone? Who did he fight for?* Of course, he then realized, *Savage probably was asking the same questions about me.*

14

Pall became fixed on the vexing problem of Savage's identity. Then the young man asked aloud, "Why didn't he just shoot me?"

The trees started thinning out more. It became lighter. Wind and rain, once again, started reaching the ground in a blowing torrent. He noticed a clearing in front of him. At the edge of its opening, he saw Savage staring straight ahead at something in the distance. Upon nearing him, Savage held out his right hand low to the ground, pushing his palm to the floor of the clearing several times.

Pall slowed down his approach. He pulled even with the other man. Savage put a finger to his own lips indicating silence. Pall took the opportunity to note that Savage towered over him.

He's got to be almost seven feet tall, he said to himself. His bow was so massive that it could be used in the service of a quarterstaff as well. Pall wanted to take time to examine him more closely, but Savage was staring so intently ahead that it forced the young warrior to focus on what it was that Savage was looking at with such concentration.

Pall saw that starting at the edge of the opening in the wood a narrow field spread out before him. It stretched out level for perhaps a hundred yards then took a slight elevation upwards. Being early spring, it was uncultivated and left to lie fallow. The section closest to him and Savage had been in the process of being fertilized. A farm house was located at the top of the rise. A barn, which was twice larger than the home, was to his right. Some hand tools that were being used for marling were still left in the field. No smoke rose from the chimney. The homestead showed the care of love and labor, yet at the same time, it felt abandoned. The sounds of nature purred around them keeping the pouring rain company. No human voices were heard. Stillness and the absence of human activity had settled thickly around the whole place.

"I don't like the feel of this place," Savage stated in a quiet undertone. "I understand that war has made all the inhabitants in this area go into hiding. But there's no one around. No stragglers. No wounded. No deserters. Not even looters, let alone squatters are here."

"Is this the same thing that you saw when you first went through here?" Pall asked.

Savage nodded a quick affirmation to the question.

"Nothing's changed from when I first saw it."

As Pall wicked away rain from his eyes with the fingers of each of his hands, he asked, "Did you look more closely at it; like go to the door or windows and look in?"

Savage shook his head no slightly.

Pall took a step to walk from the edge of the trees into the field. Savage quickly put his hand out in a

16

stopping motion without touching him. "Let's wait here a bit and watch some more."

Pall quietly asked Savage, "Is there a name to the woods we have just passed through?"

The bowman mutely looked at the young man momentarily and then stared back into the depths of the trees from which they had passed. "Yes," he barely uttered. "There are several names for this wood. It is called by some the Demesne of the Copper Beeches. The trees stand as Sentinels of the forest. A few know it as the Wood of the Royal Guard. They are sacred to many in this part of the country."

Pall did not respond to Savage's comment. Like the bowman, he looked back into the forest wistfully.

They stood before the edge of the field for about a quarter of an hour. Nothing changed around the farmhouse and grounds. It was silent but for the sounds of the weather around them. Toward the end of their observing the place, a flock of forest ravens flew across the top of the house, winging their way from the battlefield. One particularly large raven alighted onto the top of the chimney. Settling its feathers with an abrupt and final shake of its wings, it stared at the buildings surrounding the main house and out at the fields as well. Finally, turning its gaze in a full circle, it seemed to be watching the place where the two men also were standing at the forest's edge. It then preened its thick black feathers and body while peering at the barn and land around the house. The bird looked up at the sky, cocked its head and stared down into the chimney itself.

Savage and Warren looked at one another after seeing the strange bird's singular actions. Neither of them said anything aloud. Savage just widened his eyes when he looked back at the raven. The bird was staring at them as if it knew they were there. It looked back down the chimney and started a comb call. One which gave out an eerie series of hoarse sounding coos, half–caws, rattles and clicks. It was a subsong of its kind that they had never heard before.

The raven stopped its calling. Pall thought it looked right back at him. It started its coarse sound again. As it did so, it whipped its wings into the air above the house and took a fast sweeping flight right at them, keeping unnaturally low to the ground. Shimmering in a swooping flight pattern with breathtaking swiftness, it moved in its own self–generated sound. Its singular movement toward them was undaunted by the weather. It creaked like someone who was walking down an old set of wooden stairs. It flew with a silk rustling echo in a five–foot soaring wingspan. The purple sheen cast from its plumage radiated sparks of deep indigo and black as if in response to its powerful and well–timed wing motions. It was an iridescence of ill will taking aim right at them.

Within thirty feet of the men it rose to eye level, gaining speed in its attack. Ten feet away it was stopped in midair by an arrow that Savage released at it. After first hitting the bird's body, the wooden shaft passed easily through it, then seemed to jutter erratically after coming out of the other side of the bird. At that point in its trajectory, the arrow just seemed to fall flat out of the air to the ground.

The raven tumbled into the place where they were standing and landed at their feet face down. Pall went to turn it over with his foot, but Savage stopped him. Savage picked up a broken tree limb from the edge of the woods into his right hand.

"Let's take a look at what we have here," he said, as he placed the sharper end of the branch next to the bird's body. He turned the creature gently over. His expression remained neutral as he searched while standing over it, to no avail, for any visible wound.

Pall knelt down next to its right side. "How can there be no wound in it?" he asked Savage. "You shot it right out of the air. We both saw the arrow go through and fall...."

The bird's eyes popped open. There were no pupils that could be seen. They were skimmed over with what looked like cataracts. Pale blue in color, they stared directly at Pall.

It sounded a low guttural rattle, tipped its head back and forth while looking at him, and knocked out a high cachinnation, "Toc–toc–toc–toc." The bird stood up on its feet. Swaying slightly back and forth in the rain, the corvid said to Pall,

"For one so young, yet still unsprung from war,
you have yet to meet the whore of moore.
She will bite and scratch and make you crawl,
until you come to an end of the starlight's pall.
A king's heart I ate in battle where you fell.
While you lost in mind, I become fell with mine.
Take care of the secret world, not even you know.
There is some bliss there, but mostly jaded woe.
I return to my crown, while you must face down
a terror from a nightmare's dream—Scream
you will, when it comes for you, until hell itself
relents from the pull of heaven and the elf
of grief puts you onto an unknown, forgotten shelf:
Life, gloom, hail stones more, laughter, crying—
All in store of time..."

The bird lifted its wings and went to take flight away from them. Flecks of darkness inked in and out from its feathers as they made a curling motion to lift him into the air. Without realizing he had done so, Pall had his sword out. He swung at the bird.

CHAPTER FIVE

The raven moved quicker than thought itself, *Or at least as fast as the average speed of reflection on a good day of rumination,* Savage silently observed.

It escaped Pall's attempt at a mortal blow. But the tip of the sword parted the bird's left underside enough to make it bleed a lot. Pall sliced it open just above his eye level; its blood immediately ran down the weapon's fuller and dripped onto his extended right arm. The bird seemed unfazed by its grievous wound.

It laughed heartily with a deeply resounding, "Prruck–prruck–prruck–prruck."

The raven flew into the top of the trees and then called out a fading cry of, "King's blood on you now, boy; 'ware on you and those upon whom you mete out your wrath."

Pall, shaking with the aftermath of his released energy in swiping at the raven and his encounter with it, wiped off the blade on the leaves of a young oak tree. The blood started to sting his arm.

"Starting to burn you now, isn't it?" Savage asked.

Pall nodded.

"Good thing it's raining like a river," Savage said. "It'll help ease the brunt of its power."

"What was that thing?" he asked Savage.

21

"That my young friend is a Valravn," Savage responded.

The rain roared down upon them. Thunder crackled nearby in deep resonant booms. The whole forest and field seemed in motion to Pall. He closed his eyes.

"A Valravn is a supernatural bird. Its name means raven of the slain. Eating the heart of a king on a field of battle as it told us, means that it's become a terrible animal."

"Why?" asked Pall.

"Because its gained insight and intelligence into men's minds. Half–wolf, half great hound, too. It's a spiteful and bitter beast. With now the awareness of the king from whose body he's fed."

"What that malvern jabbering to me about?" Pall asked faintly. His eyes turned inwards. He lost sight of what was around him. He faded from the world.

"What is it that you want to do with yourself?" his mother asked him.

"Travel, Mom," he responded. I want to see what's around me."

"I know," she said with a sigh. "You're young, full of life and tired of this one here at the smithy."

She was tying off sage, rue and horehound on the rafters in the room next to the forge. When he looked again at the horehound she was working with, he frowned at it, as though it should have reminded him of something he had just heard. He recognized its fifteen to eighteen–inch wooly, distinctively shaped and wrinkled leaves. He knew that the small white flowers of the herb contained a bitter juice and left a nasty taste in one's mouth.

"You know, I never could figure out why that herb is given such a crazy name."

"Well," she laughed, "the second word in its formal name is vulgar."

He smiled at her repartee about what the herb was called. "Yes, you have told me its first name—Marrubium, isn't it?"

"Yes. It's excellent when made into a tea, or even a hard candy, for colds, stuffy noses, sore throats and when the lungs are filled with fluid. Sweetened with lemon juice or molasses makes it taste a lot better. It can be also used to get rid of worms in animals."

The sound of repeated hammering on iron came from the blacksmith's workshop. Occasionally, he heard the metal being quenched. Whenever his father was working with it he sang in a low, well–modulated voice. He could never clearly hear the words that his father sang. Pall thought that it was in another language; or, at least one that his dad was making up as he carburized the iron into steel suitable for the task at hand, be it the making of

23

highly sought after weapons or for tools. Pall knew that his dad loved the tools he had made because they were not only highly prized by the excellent blacksmith that he was, but by many individuals far and wide around the village where they lived. Working with finely made tools, such as specialized tongs and shatterproof hammers, allowed his father to create some of the finest steel weapons and armor many of the warriors, farmers and other craftsmen had ever seen when they visited his workshop.

His forge was a wonder to behold. The huge granite–pieced furnace and bellows were a sight to see and a sound with which to flood one's senses. Once in operation, it was mesmerizing to watch the way the fire could be shaped by the bellows in creating the right temperatures for his father to fashion whatever he was tasked to make out of the metal he was working with.

The air being blown into the fire created a waterfall like, even a tidal shifting, sound.

At the end of each long day of labor, his father would put everything back in place and make sure that the fire in the furnace was banked for the next day's work.

When Pall asked, "I understand why we don't keep the fire going through the night. But why do we go through the effort of returning all the tools to their original area of storage and cleaning up what we've done for the day? We're just going to start all over again the next day."

"I know it seems unnecessary to you, and to many other craftsmen, too," his father responded. "Yet for me, I love to end the day by putting everything back in its place. It helps clear my mind and settle me down for the evening. The next day when I return here, I begin it with a fresh start. I see things that I did not see the day before. Many of my best ideas on what I'm working on are figured out overnight. Stepping into this workspace when it's all clean the very first thing in the morning is a blessing the good Lord helps me give myself."

He continued to watch his mother work at hanging the herbs. He felt that something was at odds with what he was watching. He could not put it together right. While he was in the moment, he felt that he was also viewing it from an outside source. As though it was a memory he was living through again.

"How can you name a plant both whore and hound?" he asked somewhat irritably.

"Well, dear, the first part of the word isn't about a strumpet, it means gray."

"So, why not call it greyhound, instead?" he asked in a half joking way. Common people were forbidden to own, or even have, such animals. Only nobles and royals could keep and maintain them.

The nobility even had to have permission from the King to own and breed any. They were incredible hunters and it was a capital offense to kill one.

"Pall, you're onto something here, maybe."

"What do you mean?"

She smiled again at him and at what they were discussing. Then again, his stepmother always seemed to be smiling. Doing so made her beauty even that more enchanting and dear to him. "This plant," as she wound twine securely around the stems of a group of horehound leaves, "being a member of the mint family has two kinds we can use for medicine. One is white and the other is black."

"Seems simple enough," he said, "for good and bad purposes."

"No, son, it's not as simple as that—but the black form, which may be why the plant is given its name, was once known to cure the bite of an older mad dog or wolf."

He heard his father stop hammering on the anvil. The sound of the last strike on the iron seemed to ring in his ears forever. He looked at his mother and she was staring at him with a worried look....

"Pall," Savage asked, while shaking him by his shoulders.

"Pall, are you going to be all right?"

He looked up at the older man. He saw the concern on his face. "What happened?"

Savage reviewed the last several moments with the raven and about the blood falling onto his right arm after Pall had struck it with his sword. "You dropped to the ground like a bunch of wet rags."

"I don't remember falling down," he said to Savage. "Indeed, I thought I lost you. A Valravn's blood is potent and lethal. Good thing it's raining as bad as it is. Helped wash a lot of it off you."

Pall saw that Savage had propped him up against a tree fall. "How long was I out?" he asked.

"Not long," Savage said. Then he smiled, adding, "Maybe 100 barrels of water fell on us while you were gone." He paused. "Did you see anything?"

"Mmmmmnn," Pall replied. "I was back home with my mother and father."

"What were you doing there?" Savage asked.

"Talking about herbs, whores and hounds."

Savage looked at him skeptically. "I think we need to get you and me out of this weather." He looked over at the farmyard. "Let's get inside and see if we can get a fire going."

Pall stood, shook himself and tentatively started walking the length of the field towards the house with Savage. It was getting towards the end of daylight.

Pall was about to take another step with his right leg when Savage exclaimed, "Phewww, will you look at that!"

Just below where he would have placed his foot was the arrow that Savage had shot at the raven. Pall picked it up. The arrow was missing its three feathers. The wood was, if possible, withered and blanched as though it had been dunked and kept in a vat of acid for a long time. They exchanged glances with one another. Neither one mentioned the raven; nor, rather, the Valravn, again. The fading light of day faintly shone off the outside walls of the farmer's home. The rain sounded as though it was sizzling off of everything it hit. The wind died out, along with the thunder and lightning.

Their footfalls echoed off the land around the dwelling. Like the rain's odd percussive boiling, their steps had a shuffling echo to them. They did not so much walk into the home as patter in with the hum of insects and with the tiredness of the bone weary.

Savage gestured at a rough, handmade rocker next to the hearth, "Have a seat and get comfortable. Let me see if I can get that fire going warm enough to take the chill out of the place."

Savage took a metal poker from the side of the fireplace. He stabbed at the fire several times. Taking a quick appraisal of the state of the ashes, he saw that there were just enough embers left glowing

Varying ages. Varying temperaments. Varying thoughts on raiding places like the one they were approaching quickly, despite their antics and camaraderie with one another. A score and a half of varying souls. Some liked taking things for their own delight. Some liked to burn. Others to pillage and rape. It did not matter either way on what was pillaged and who was raped. They were divided in style. They were united in destroying whatever they touched, tossed and tortured when on their hunt for spoils. They stopped in front of the path into the farm.

A tall man in dark green, standing next to a man of similar height and dressed in light gray, smiled slightly. "Well, men, let's see what we have to play with here."

A few of the men laughed easily. After he entered the path and began striding quickly down it, everyone else followed. They pulled through the opening gate in one gulp of motion.

They were quieter now. Smaller groups of men peeled off from the main one. They had done this before, many times. Each had an assigned role and task to follow. All torches were snuffed out.

———+—

Pall stirred from his reverie. He frowned. Instead of feeling rested, he felt even more exhausted than when he first sat down in front of the hearth. His heart beat rapidly. He stood. His right hand firmly gripped the pommeled hilt of his sword. Pall forced himself to relax, especially his breathing. He listened for ten full breaths.

Hearing nothing out of hand, he cautiously approached the entrance to the house. He momentarily stood on the door's threshold. He stepped into the yard.

Two pairs of hands grabbed both of his shoulders and arms. A third huge pair grabbed him roughly by the neck. He was pushed and pulled back into the room he had just left. Forced into the rocking chair he had just got up from, three men stared back at him.

A fourth individual, dressed all in green and whom he had not seen before, held Pall's sword with practiced ease by the hilt. Like Savage before him in this room, he solicitously said, "Why don't you sit down there and get comfortable."

Unlike Savage, he pointed the sword at the center of Pall's chest. He pressed the point slightly, firmly, against him. Nothing was said. Pall looked at him. The man's companions all looked at Pall.

Soon, the tall man in gray walked, sauntered, into the room. More to himself than anyone present in the room, he slightly asked, yet boldly stated, "What do we have here, my pretty."

The large, fat man next to him snickered slightly. He was dressed in mustard–yellow garb. "This one looks like we can have some sport with!" He winked at Pall.

Pall saw that this fellow must have been the one who had almost throttled him by the throat.

The fat one smacked his lips and flicked his tongue out at Pall. "Tasty, I'd say!"

Ironically, he saw that the two men, who had grabbed him by the sides, were identical twins. Their clothes were nondescript. They looked like they had swathed muddy rags around their bodies in a wet anger.

The leader in green said, softly, "You didn't answer my question, boy."

Pall looked at him steadily, saying, "You made a statement, not a question."

The twins simultaneously sucked in an audible breath. Their hands gripped him tighter.

The man in green said, "True enough."

Pall heard more men around him. Some were in other parts of the house. Some were talking quietly to one another directly outside the front door. Others, he felt, were nearby.

I wonder where Savage is?

He heard laughter.

"Let's have a proper introduction to one another," the man holding Pall's sword said to him. I am called Error. Not that I make mistakes;" he smiled mockingly, "people I meet think it was their fault life put them in my hands. Thus, they met their Error." He stopped talking, looked at his prisoner in the rocking chair, waiting for a response to his introducing himself to Pall.

The young man waited a bit, then said, "My name is Pall— with a double L."

"Lovely," the man rejoined, "with such a name as that, I will be your dismay." Upon making this comment, the man in gray took Pall's sword away from Error.

More men came into the farmer's home. Some had food. Some had drink. Others brought their varied and sundry appetites for fun, fight and food alike into the house.

Supper was quickly made, while the five men encircling Pall went about their interrogation undisturbed.

The fire seemed to burn brighter and emitted an unusual amount of heat.

The gray man held the young soldier's sword up against the light of the fire and stared at it with undisguised admiration over its weight, balance and workmanship. He hefted it with accomplished ease and struck a fighting stance in front of Pall. The men nearby melted away against the walls of the room.

The gray man took a series of offensive head and body strikes at Pall, holding back within an inch of hitting him each time the blade came flashing in at the young man.

Pall stood stock still, but wavered slightly on his feet. The exertions, wounds, and exhaustion of the day overwhelmed him.

Error became vexed over the young man's stoicism, especially in the face of the gray man's feigned, but alarmingly vicious, attack against him. Taking advantage of Pall's weariness and near fatigue, Error spun away from Pall and came back at him with a chest high kick to the middle of his body. Pall was knocked violently against the outer wall of the room.

While he slowly got back onto his feet, everyone in the room watched him do so without comment.

The gray man's sword practice against Pall resumed. Faster now. Superficially touching the soldier's body with the falchion's exquisitely sharp point.

With a final flourish, the sword stopped right up against the young man's flesh. The gray man then pressed its point further into Pall's solar plexus. It began to break the skin. Pall could feel blood start to flow slightly around the tip of his weapon.

"Where does a farm boy like you get such a fine weapon as I now hold against you?" the man in gray asked him with a grating curiosity.

Pall looked steadily at the man without saying anything.

"The beat up warrior's outfit that you're wearing, you filch it off a dead soldier, boy?" Error asked with contempt.

Pall remained quiet.

"Is this your da's place, son?" the man in gray asked as the sword was pressed against Pall more firmly.

Pall carefully and slightly shook his head as to say, "No."

"What are you doing here?" Error asked.

"Same as you, Error," Pall answered.

"Wrong!" Error exclaimed. "You've made five mistakes already. And I barely know you."

The twins and Error grabbed Pall and pushed him into the rocking chair. The man in gray kept the pressure of the sword held against Pall's chest as he was moved to a seated position.

The fat one in mustard said, "First, you were born."

In order of one then another, the first twin said, "Second, you're alive."

The other twin remarked, "Third, in front of us you are held."

Error did not add to the count, but said, indicating the man in gray, "He has your blade in his hands."

The gray man smiled disdainfully. He concluded the listed sarcasm, saying, "Fifth, his name's Master Error to you, boy."

Almost indiscernibly, the blade eased its pressure held against him. Error said to someone else in the adjoining room, "Get some rope. Get em out of the chair. Truss em up tight. Sacrifice position."

A rope was quickly obtained and handed to Mustard. The fat man tied Pall's hands and feet together, first placing them behind Pall's back.

"Ohhh," he crooned, "I'm getting to like this even more."

The other end of the rope was securely wound around the young man's neck.

The gray man, now standing with right hand akimbo, and with the palm of his left hand on the end of the hilt, disdainfully forced the sword's point into the floorboard.

The blade remained swaying slightly to and fro, a makeshift pendulum vibrating to an altered sense of time. When the sword had been stuck into the floor, Pall felt as though it had struck him as well. The world itself was swaying back and forth in front of him.

"Put him into the nearest corner here where the firelight shines the closest," the man in gray instructed before he summarily left the farmhouse.

Pall was lifted up and dumped roughly into said corner.

Master Error, without showing any emotion, looked around him. Remaining silent, he momentarily watched Pall's sword sway side to side several times. Much to his men's relief, he soon followed the man in gray and left the room.

The first twin ambiguously cautioned Pall, "Be careful," he warned.

The second twin said, "Yeah, you don't wanna strangle yourself."

Mustard informed him to keep his neck, back and legs arched. "Otherwise, you choke to death. But I'll be your watcher for the shift in the night when you get real tired. Just before you're played out, I'll be sure to tire you out some more," he gestured lewdly at himself. He laughed in delight: "You and me will get on just nice," he added with relish. "Specially for me." He paused in his exaggerated ecstasy, then said, "Nnnnnnnnn, not so much you, though, which will make me enjoy our dance together even more."

Mustard man said to First and Second, the names that Pall had instinctively given to each of the twins, "I'm third shift. Be sure to wake me up and let me know if he's startin not to breathe."

With that command to the twins made, he walked enough distance away from Pall to go to sleep, but close enough into position to be able to open his eyes and watch Pall's condition throughout the night.

Pall initially tried to get comfortable, which was truly impossible to do. He had to make sure that his back and legs remained as close together as he was able to get them. But it could not be done. The pain he soon experienced quickly became intolerably severe. He soon realized that he had to keep the full tension of the rope off his neck. It was not an easy thing to accomplish. As the night wore on, it became more difficult to do. Sweat poured off him as he fought to stay conscious and alive.

His wounds from fighting earlier that morning were plaguing him more now that he was in one fixed position. The burn he received from the blood of the Valravn on his right arm started anew. It stung him with a sparkling intensity that added to his affliction in being hogtied. Also, the recently inflicted sword wound to his chest added to his overall weakened condition.

Eventually, the men finished their meal and settled down for the night. Some of them were assigned as lookouts and placed in the main room. Some were put outside the entrance. Others were strategically positioned throughout the farmstead. They were working in three shifts throughout the rest of the night.

The fire burned down during the next several hours. When the first shift changed over to the next one, Second put several more logs on the hot embers. Flames sprouted eagerly around the new fuel.

Pall was now having trouble making sense of what was happening to him. He became angry. At the men around him. At the plight he was in. At himself for not remembering who he was at the moment. The rope secured so tightly on him became an extension of the fire. The tautness of the knots Mustard had tied on him burned into his arms, legs and neck, just as the wooden knots in the hearth seared into flickering light. To make things even worse, his stomach was growling. He could not recall that he had anything to eat that whole day. For that matter, he had no idea when he had last had a meal at all. His feet, legs, hands and arms, in turn, felt on fire.

He and the fire became one. A memory flared in his mind.

He was fourteen years of age. He was line fishing. The early morning sun shone with a sweet brightness of youth. At the edge of a glade, and before him in the creek, was one of his favorite places to be. A deep pool, breathtakingly clear to the bottom, faced him. He knew at this time of day trout were just underneath the overhang of a shelf of granite rocks at the far side of the pool. The current hardly pulled at this point in the brook.

He had brought two poles with him, one being a short line, or snood, and the other a long line. Because the trout he was after were about fifteen feet away and five to eight feet down in the water, he was going to be long lining. He had several secret weapons. One was a specially made cork for floating the line with the hook attached at the end. He had made this float by hand carving it from a larger piece. The cork had been given to his father as part payment for a fishing spear and for a sword that he had made for a foreign warrior from the Western Isles.

The man's name was Nua. He was heavily tattooed and spoke Paul's language with a thick, guttural accent. Most of what the man said to him was barely comprehensible. Pall remembered that Nua was very proud of the cork, and that the older man called it "Corcaigh". Pall never could get the pronunciation right, despite trying to say it many times with Nua's brusque encouragement.

"It's in my people's old tongue, boyo," he told Pall. "It means marsh in your words," he explained to Pall when he had asked the strangely tattooed man what the word corcaigh meant.

Another invaluable tool was the reel his father had fashioned for him in the smithy. It had a finely tooled winder that helped bring in the line without requiring the labor to bring it in hand over hand. It meant a lot to Pall that his father trusted him enough that he could fish on his own with this gear. Pall had to be attentive, though, in using the reel. If he was not careful the meticulously wrought, horsehair line could get all twisted up and entangle itself inside it. Often the line might be lost because it would have to be cut out of the reel. After so much use, he would take it off the reel and straighten any kinks that might have gotten in the line.

He had two types of line fishing rods. Both were made out of hazel wood. The six–foot rod was made from a single shoot obtained and cut from a hedge earlier that morning. He was very proud of the long line rod, it had taken him extra care and time in creating it. It was of gnarled, twisted hazel, and supple enough to dance to the pulling and bending of a caught fish on the other end of the line. The long line rod, being fourteen feet in length, felt magical in his grip. Sometimes, he would practice dry land swings, not so much to perfect the method of casting, but just to hear the swish and swoosh of the wood moving in the air around him. He would often imitate the sound in a low whistle while doing so.

He often fished with a worm or two on the hook; however, in fishing at this spot this morning, he was going to use a fake fly that his mother first taught him to make for such an occasion. The lure he was going to use was one made from a bright red, cardinal feather as well as from a piece of wild boar bristle.

He started working on a knot to secure the line to the tip of the rod. Instead of using the reel, he felt it would simply be better to cast the line in a pick-up–and–lay–down motion. For some reason, he could not get the knot tied correctly. He discovered that he was unable to untie the knot he had made. This was frustrating. He wanted to be fishing, not sweating over knots. He began to be tormented by the effort to get it undone....

A deep craving for water brought his senses back to the place where he was tied. He was at the beginning of a painful journey he did not want to think about. Emerging out of visions from his past, he shied away from the thought of entering the present. As reality pushed its way into his awareness, he jounced back and forth on the floor of the farmhouse kitchen. An image came to his mind. He felt like a stallion. Proud. Independent.

Consciousness had arrived to tame him, a rider of terrible force with a whip of agony set on conquering his spirit. He bunched his muscles underneath him and bucked violently away from this specter of a horseman.

He heard himself stamping the ground with four powerful hooves; he shredded the soil apart with a bitter and acrid anger. Thick clouds of dirt and dried muck were churned into the air. Long, ghostly looking tatters of dust swirled around where he stood. Yet he became confused at the same time: wooden boards were underneath him not soil.

The ache for something to drink was filling his senses. Pain was present, but his whole body had gone numb. He heard himself alternately panting aloud and moaning.

He opened his eyes and saw Second add a few logs to the fire. When he was done doing so, Second slapped his hands against his upper thighs. He saw that Pall was looking at him. "Comfortable?" Second queried him with a snort of derision.

He went over to Pall and tested the tension on the rope. Second jerked hard on it several times with both of his hands. Waves of renewed agony from the position Pall was in coursed through him. It was as though the lightning outside and the fire in the hearth had somehow gotten into his body and were stinging him with thousands of sharp bites. A deep sigh of misery escaped from his throat.

Second looked up from his task in checking Pall's being tied well.

The gray man walked into the room. He looked at Second briefly, then inquired at both of them, "So, how's our guest doing?"

"He's cooin like a mornin dove, Mordant," Second said with a satisfied chuckle.

"No names here, lad," he cautioned Second. "Then, I suppose it doesn't matter with this one," indicating Pall. He bent down on his knees and eyed Pall directly. "Though I don't think it matters much. You'll be gone soon from the look of you. Gregor Mordant's my full name. Pleased to meet you more formally this time."

"It's a pleasure to meet your acquaintance," Pall managed to get out in response.

Mordant, looking surprised, than delighted, beamed with a smile. "I like the feisty answer; Pall is it?"

Pall nodded, then gasped as a spasm of anguish overwhelmed him.

"You have obviously met some of my men. We call ourselves Mordant's Marauders. We live off the spoils of war; and, congratulations, you're one of them: plunder that is. And, you will be spoiled." He paused in his introductory statement, as if waiting for Pall to say something.

Pall closed his eyes. He drew air into his lungs through brief shallow breaths, then said, "Thought Master Error was the leader."

"He would like to think so," Mordant agreed. "He's my captain. I try to give him his head," he said as he made a quick, horizontal gesture across the front of his neck.

Looking at Second, Mordant said to him, "Send one of the guards to get me if the young master's condition becomes, shall we say, critical? I have a few more questions for him. And, don't let Gordo get too playful with him at first," he added, referring to Mustard.

"But, your Honor," Second grumbled, "I want to get some sleep, not stay up and watch the fat one play."

"Shut up, and do what I'm telling you to, Twin," Mordant commanded. As he went out the door to the yard outside, he told Second, now known as Twin, to pull on Pall's rope more vigorously and to double check that it was still tightly binding him.

Making sure Mordant was out of sight and hearing, Twin swore profusely. He cursed over the fact that he had to guard this stupid victim. He uttered obscenities at Pall. And he damned the task that he had to oversee in watching the sick, fat one watch, or torture, Pall. Twin reached down and gave a merciless pull on the rope.

Pall was pulled back into the previous memory of his going fishing.

———┼—

Savage stood back up after finishing his appraisal of the farmer and his family's bodies. He turned around just at the same time that he heard several voices at the front of the barn. Sheet lightning bleached the scene at the door's entrance. Three men were lit up in silhouette. In black, cut out against a wall of light, he could not determine who they were or what they had on them for weapons.

"You stay here until I relieve you," he heard one of them say.

When lightning flashed again, Savage could see that one remained standing just inside the doorway. The bowman picked a place in the loft where he could sit down and not be seen and still observe the sentry before him. He checked that his bowstring was dry. He took a soft cloth out that was in his pack. Wiping the drawstring down and up and down again, he placed an arrow alongside his right hand.

The rain remained relentless in its downpour around the farmstead.

———┼—

"Pall Warren," his stepmother admonished him, "Are you bringing something to eat with you while you are out fishing today?" she accused, more than asked, him. "I have some bread and cheese," he said to her.

"Here, I remade your pack. I added some almonds and a cup to drink from in the stream."

A terrible spasm shot through him.

His memory flooded forward in time.

He had been fishing now for several hours. The wind was just right for him not to be seen by the fish underneath. The surface of the brook ruffled in timed response to the motion of the breeze. The sun stood just past its highest point in the sky. Pall's shadow did not fall over the area where he was angling. Two large, multihued trout had already been caught, gutted and set within the stream on a separate line nearby to keep them fresh.

He wanted to catch one more. He approached the place that he thought was the best one to fish. It was in the deep end of the pool. There was a spot underneath the rocks where trout liked to stay and float in the coolness of its shaded area. It was also further underneath the granite outcropping in the water. He had dived down and explored that area every summer since he was a young boy. He knew it well.

At this moment, he felt himself go through a massive physical change.

Before he could completely understand what had happened to him, he noticed he was hovering in an aqueous fluid just above the graveled streambed with his other trout companions. He looked out with wariness underneath the granite cleft in the stream, watching what the stream brought him for food. Staying in place with a slight movement of his fins, Pall could see the banks of the stream and the surface of the water. He felt the blue sky over him. The sounds in the water that he heard were like home to him. They filled him with power and deep contentment.

An errant mayfly spinner was blown onto the surface of the water. It struggled in its circle of impact. The insect's transparent wings beat a rhythm of concentric ripples outward from where it had become trapped. He was hungry now, not just curious about observing his surroundings. The mayfly's struggles sharpened his appetite to the point that nothing else mattered. He had to eat this tasty morsel. He rose to the top of the brook and set the insect into his lower jaw.

Suddenly, something sharp bit into the roof of his mouth. He fled away, down into the bottom of the stream bed in swift panic. Just as his first spurt of speed pushed him into the pull of the current, he felt himself being brought up and out of the water. Pall smacked the water's surface powerfully with his tail fins. He was lifted into the air. He gasped in complete shock as it fully engulfed his awareness.

Mustard was grunting with the effort of picking Pall up by the shoulders. Failing to do so, the big man dragged him closer to the fire, making sure not to knock Pall's sword over where it still remained embedded point first into the floor.

The fat man held tightly onto the rope in the junction between where Pall's arms and legs were tied together.

"Ahhhh, what a present I have for me here," he grunted in cheerful effort.

Pall opened his eyes and saw the fat man grinning evilly back at him. He tried to say something, but all he could *muster for the mustard one*, he thought, was a series of croaks and dry coughs.

"Twin," Mustard said to him, "fetch my mercykiller I just left on the table there. And," he paused, "while you're at it, open the shutters to the window. It's gotten too hot in here for close work with him," the fat one indicated over to Pall with his thumb.

Twin sighed in frustration at having to be an unwilling witness to what was happening to Pall.

As Twin went, first, to take care of the sole window into the room, he said to himself, *I could be somewheres a lot nicer than here, and having something good to drink, too.*

He reached out to the handles on the slatted shutters, grabbed them in turn and closed both together, but not tightly. He left them standing at a slight angle apart from one another before the window frame. *I'm not going to give this fool of an exceedingly fat cow the satisfaction of shutting them.*

Twin turned away from the window. Despite his feeling disgusted with the situation he once again had to look at in front of him, he walked over to the table and brought back an evil looking dagger to Mustard. Twin handed over a long, thin-bladed knife to the man in yellow.

"That's a good man," said Mustard, as he took the proffered weapon hilt first into his right hand.

A part of Pall, which was able to watch this transaction, recognized that the kind of knife Mustard now had in his hand was formally known as a *misericorde*. It was used to give a death, or mercy, stroke in dispatching men who were mortally wounded in combat. It also could be effectively employed at close quarters when grappling with an opponent. He felt an anticipation of relief that perhaps Mustard was going to kill him.

Pall finally would be released from what seemed now to be a life of hardship, injury and torture.

Mustard looked at him kindly, though Pall knew it was not with empathy. "Well see here: we're gonna do some slight tailorin of your garments, so I can get at you easier."

Having had his leather armor removed from him before he was tied, the young man now had on a light woolen tunic. Mustard proceeded to slice it off Pall's body in three long slashes of the knife. Next, the fat man cut away Pall's undershirt. The knife being cruelly sharp, slit through the woven flax garment with ease.

Mustard stood back to appraise his work. "Much nicer," he said. "Now don't you feel better, boy?" he asked.

Savage had patiently waited until the second sentry was being replaced with his relief. At that moment, when the guard was being changed, the two men involved skipped any pretense of formality in doing so. Not caring about such military niceties, they remained on station talking with one another.

The bowman silently stood up.

Lightning still flickered around them, illuminating the men intermittently.

Savage waited until the third strike struck above in the night sky.

Their conversation completed, the man ending his shift walked away. In doing so, he had to step in front of his replacement. Savage adjusted an arrow to his bow and raised both evenly at the other two men. He pulled himself thoroughly into the horns of the bow stave. A sharp light ignited the air. With the bow fully drawn and aimed, Savage released the arrow. It dove unerringly straight into the neck of the remaining sentry and through him with the ease of parting a warm piece of butter in half. The man gargled a response to the arrow's flight into him to no avail, particularly in bringing attention to the danger he was just experiencing. He folded into the ground in a single fall toward the other Marauder. The arrow ploughed into the second man's back and, except for the feathers, all but cleared his chest. He sank to his knees in the rain.

The bowman cleared the loft and ladder with ease and went to inspect the damage he had just wrought. Starting to walk through the barn to the entryway, he stopped immediately upon hearing the brief call of a wood thrush. The call of the thrush was an abbreviated one. There was no flute–like phrase in its song that Savage was familiar with in listening to a thrush sing in the forest. No variation to its call was given. A soft trill started, "Prit–prit–prit," and repeated. He then heard what sounded like the aggressive snapping of the bird's jaws.

A large bird. Not likely one from the size of a thrush.

This signature call had a particular and disturbing stridency to it. It was a mock signal never made by mandibles belonging to a bird.

Successively rapid pulses clicked and chittered ominously away.

Sweat broke out on his forehead. The hairs on the back of his neck moved. His shoulders felt as if wolf spiders were skittering along them. He knew this voice. It did not come from a bird. Goose bumps sprung up on his arms. Savage backed underneath the loft. He hid amongst the tack and blankets of a horse that was not there in the barn with him.

As a matter of fact, he thought to himself, t*here aren't any farm animals around at all. Haven't been since I first set my eyes on this place.*

Lightning flashed again and he saw what appeared to be the liquid outlines of a panther that transformed back and forth into an immense snake. But this creature stood up on its end. It did not just crawl along the ground on its belly. The beast did not seem to have the solidity of a real animal. It blotched back and forth morphing from shape to shape. At times, it appeared to have a snout braced with wicked looking upper and lower teeth. It moved low to the ground, crab walking over to the first sentry who had been shot through the neck. The thing was translucent. It shifted into a shimmering pattern of silver outlines.

Rain fell on everything outside of the confines of the dead farmer's barn. Except upon the creature thirty feet in front of Savage.

Mustard grasped his mercygiver by the blade. He ran the hilt alongside Pall's backbone. From the base of the spine to the neck, and back again twice, saying, "I think you and me are going to get right cozy with each other."

Mustard untied the knots on the rope.

At first, Pall felt nothing happen. All too quickly, feeling started to come back, and then cascaded into him in a waterfall, a torrent of affliction.

Pall managed to grunt at Mustard. The young man was ramped into a series of convulsions. Arched on his back on the floor, the heels of his leather boots beat out a staccato rhythm of suffering.

Mustard somersaulted the knife hilt back into his grip. He pressed the blade into Pall's lower back. He smiled wickedly at Pall. The thinly shaped knife point went into his flesh about a half inch.

Pall gasped aloud, shouting, "The Lord's mercy be upon me!"

"There's no quarter given you here by the God above, except for what's in my hand right now." Mustard shifted his position and braced himself to place the knife deeper into the young man.

Twin went over to Mustard and pled with him to stop. "You're goin too fast. Slow down. Mordant wants the lad to be hale enough to be queried by Error."

"I'll do what I want to this worm, Twin," he spat. "He's mine to do what I will to him."

As Twin walked out of the room to fetch the sentry standing outside the farmhouse door, Mustard stood up. He looked at Pall. Wearing a blank face, Mustard kicked Pall in the side of the left temple with the toe of his right boot.

Pall gasped into the light and hot air of a summer day. He had been fishing here he remembered. Yet, there was no evidence of his fishing equipment or even of the fish he had caught anywhere nearby. He was walking further upstream alongside the brook. The stream became smaller and narrower as he proceeded to follow the course of the water. He found himself in a large, open meadow through which the brook meandered in widening loops. At one point, the brook became just a shallow puddle. The ground on all sides around it pinched the water into an hourglass shape. To get across this juncture in the water, he was faced with either walking around it, or fording across.

Pall stepped into the water. He thought he would be placing his feet in a depth no more than a half a foot. Instead, he was shocked when he discovered that he had walked into a pool of water that was way over his head. He did not have a chance to catch his breath. Choking from the effort of trying to come back out into the air, he kicked powerfully with his feet, while moving his hands and arms to help propel him upwards as fast as he could do so.

He broke the surface of the water. Taking deep breaths of relief, he saw that everything had changed around him. The shape of the puddle had turned into a large stream. He found himself in the middle, treading water to keep his head above its surface.

In the distance, about five hundred paces away from him, he discerned a black–clad and boat–like shape floating downstream at him. First appearing as a small dot that was almost similar to a silver ha'penny, it transformed itself into the size of a groat, or large silver coin, and then gained in size to the larger shape of one of the king's commemorative, sovereign marks. It was like nothing he had ever seen on the water. Inexorable in its steadfast approach towards him, it gained in bulk and mass until it loomed over him in a huge rectangular form. It was death in the water coming at him. If it touched him, Pall knew he would die.

The creature that Savage saw was familiar to him by reputation only. Rumors of it had reached him. He also had come across evidence of its ravaging people and animals several times before in his assignments. Part of his designated duties, for the crown and the king's minister of affairs to whom he reported, was to gather more information about similar sightings and activities as the one he was currently exposed to now. He was also ordered not to interfere with any encounters with such creatures and/or entities, but to observe and to take note of the details associated with them.

He knew its name, at least the one given to it by his people. It was called Ünger. At the moment, it appeared to be thoroughly "snuffling" the body of the first man Savage had just shot in the neck, as if it were a horse drawing air into its nose to appraise the barley or hay it was about to eat. Ünger, now seemingly satisfied with its initial sniffing, moved to the next man and went through the same meticulous process of inspection, alternately changing into its three shapes of panther, snake and lizard while it did so.

The creature moved apart from both men's bodies, reallocating the space in front of the barn's doorway in one swift fluid motion. It reared itself up in the form of a snake and looked deeply into the confines of the barn.

Savage held his breath. He knew he was defenseless before its presence. The best information he had about being face to face with Ünger in such a predatory situation was to become a neutral part of his surroundings. He forced himself not to think of anything. He made himself visualize a favorite spot in which he liked to hunt. He shoved his outside awareness into this image.

Ünger gave its wood thrush call that Savage had previously heard. It stood still for a span of at least a hundred heartbeats. The bowman could feel its presence, animate with a vile hatred against any living thing, trying to manipulate him, or anything else living in the barnyard area, to reveal itself. Swaying back and forth in slow motion, Ünger chirped several more times. It looked back at the bodies of the dead men on the ground. Its own body stopped swaying back and forth. It went completely still.

The bowman kept his eyes closed during this time. Had he kept them opened he would have portrayed his presence to the creature. Its bearing was too powerful. Any other creature in its vicinity would panic. It took exceptional willpower for a man to ignore it. The force of its dread might made most living things betray their fear to it.

Savage tamped down the amplitude of his life force.

Ünger gurgled a string of light chirps and cricket sounds. Again, it began swaying side to side. Remaining in its snake form, and much to Savage's relief, it slithered back to the sentry who was first shot by Savage.

In its serpentine guise, Ünger placed itself lengthwise on top of the dead man. The beast clicked its jaws together in a sharp, rapid chatter, a hurried fibrillation filled with wanton hunger. Ünger's snapping sounded more like a butcher wielding a cleaver against a carcass. It was as though Savage was listening to meat being sliced through with a fascinating ease of movement. He could even hear the accompanying chunk and whack of the blade as it snicked into place onto the hollow cutting board underneath the body.

An unbidden reaction spilled into his mind. *It's beyond a far cry from the warning given off in anger by an innocent bird.*

The creature entwined itself with the corpse. In garish effect, all the more pronounced by the sheet lightning, the demon noisily inhaled the fluids, brain, heart, lungs, eyes, teeth and blood, as well as the rest of the former sentry's complete viscera from his body cavity.

While the snake part of Ünger stayed in place consuming the body, the panther and lizard part separated from it. They ripped away from the engorged serpent, and rippled out into the open. Emanating a feral light of their own, they flickered in and out of sight. Silver glints flashed along with the lightning. Thunder rolled far away. Conjoined, but separate, with one another as well, the double-creature looked fully around the scene. Two heads took in the area. One sniffing. The other flicking its forked tongue. It undulated and shifted smoothly over to stand above the second sentry's body.

Transfixed and horrified by what he was witnessing, Savage stayed in place. He had not known that the demon could split itself apart like it just did before his eyes. He assumed that Ünger was simply one foul entity. Not a three-in-one monster.

He watched in awe as the second corpse rose in the air. Gradually, it was turned over on its back. Its arms dropped down by its sides. Blood dripped onto the arrow and then pooled off of it onto the ground. Its face was turned toward the opening of the barn door. Due more to the force of gravity, and with the body face down, the arrow fell away into the muck.

CHAPTER SEVEN

Mordant, having rested for a while, sent for Error. The green man appeared right away after being summoned to the Marauders' leader.

"I want you to head south before dawn," Mordant told him, "and hook up with our friends in Gullswater."

"Yes, Sire," Error responded.

Both men looked out toward the darkness. They could hear the wind sighing in the trees nearby. "Dawn will be here soon," Error softly said.

Mordant nodded, "Yes, and just before the sun rises I want you to do some reconnaissance for us. You're to skirt the eastern edge of the recent battlefield and look for any signs of a military presence. I don't care which side it is, as long as you report it properly to our brethren there. I think the King's forces were completely crushed. But runners must have been sent back and forth between them and the Crown's military commanders. The attack today was not on the main force, but one involving an ancillary one, part of the King's elite guard."

"If I see something of interest to us, do you want me to investigate the particulars of it more?" asked Error.

Mordant looked sharply at his captain, saying to him, "Use your best judgment, Error; but, pay particular attention at how the forces of either side, or both, are dispersed. What are the conditions of the men, their morale, fighting spirit, weapons, uniform markings, command leadership, units involved... the usual."

"I'm sure you want me to see how they are being supplied as well," Error commented, more than asked.

Mordant nodded in agreement with Error's statement. "I'll be sure to mark out civilian and monastic activity, too," Error said.

"Fine, Captain, you need to get prepared to go. We'll meet up with you in about a week or two," Gregor summarily said. He dismissed Error to the green man's preparations for leaving on his scouting mission.

Lightning flared. Feeling restless, he walked away from the outbuilding. He listened carefully for any other sounds other than the rain solely pouring down. Hearing nothing untoward, he hunched his shoulders against the wind and the rain. Mordant went to check on the rest of his men.

As luck, or perhaps fate, would have it, Mordant walked in the opposite direction of Ünger and Savage's location. Thus, he did not immediately become involved in the mayhem that was now occurring in front of the barn. Even though he had placed three, two-man patrols around the perimeter of the property they were in, none had yet discovered what was happening in its center. To be sure, Mordant thought it odd that the farmer, his family and all their livestock were missing. It was one of his concerns about which he wanted to question Pall. The young man did not have the looks or markings of a farmer, especially in his military bearing and, even more so, with the superb quality of the sword he carried. The condition of the uniform and armor Pall had worn looked tailor made for him, regardless of its condition from being in a pitched battle. He was the only human being, living that is, he and his men had come across for half a day.

There was, in addition, something not right with the young man. He seemed uncomfortable and uneasy, unsure of whom he was supposed to be. However, the Commander did not think these outward behaviors were indicative of what was disturbing him about Pall.

Perhaps, the sword was something he had come across and taken from the field of battle.

Gregor frowned at that speculation.

If he hadn't taken it as a souvenir, and if he isn't a local native, just what is he?

The Commander was irritated that he could not decipher who this young man was, at least in this small scheme of events currently taking place around the farm. He wondered if Pall knew about, or had anything to do with, this place and its inhabitants.

Mordant looked at the rain coming down on him during a sustained moment of flickering light. Thunder rolled and boomed off in the distance.

He thought he would start checking with the men patrolling the area from, coincidentally, where Savage and Pall had first seen the farmstead.

⸻

Error, after a perfunctory conversation with one of the sentries outside the farmhouse, walked towards the smokehouse, which was on the far side of the barn where he was staying for the night. The green man was feeling particularly out of humor this evening. Nothing seemed right to him. Hence, Error thought it odd when he heard what sounded to him like the call of a wood thrush.

Here it is, chirping late at night in the middle of a rotten storm.

He didn't like it. Something wasn't right. None of his men would make such a sound.

This storm probably woke the damned bird up and it can't sleep like me, he bellyached to himself.

Notwithstanding his moodiness, his sense of the disposition of his men remained honed to a sharp edge of awareness.

He made a silent tally of their locations: *Twelve men are sleeping in a row of sheds directly opposite from the farmhouse. Five men are guarding the farmhouse proper, two in front, with one each on the other three sides. Twin and the fat one are with the prisoner in the farmhouse. The Commander is in one of the bedrooms. Six men are patrolling the areas around us. Two men are....*

His reckoning was interrupted as a bolt of lightning struck a tall tree about fifty feet away from the other side of the barn. The top third of the tree was sheared off from the bolt. The light from the strike seemed to hold his attention for a long time, longer than he thought was prudent once he was able to take in the scene before him. He scrutinized the damage done to the tree and where part of it fell onto the ground.

Feeling that he was being unnecessarily distracted by the force of nature occurring just in front of him, Error started looking fully around his location. He saw, with increasing surprise, and then alarm, one man down on the ground and being consumed by what looked like a very large snake. The body of a second man was just settling on its back in the middle of the air. Next to it stood an unnerving looking apparition. It not only shifted back and forth in and out of sight, it also switched, likewise, from being a panther to a lizard of some horrendous kind.

Without thinking, he plunged away from the scene. He headed where twelve of his companions were sleeping. A part of him also hoped that one of the patrols was nearby so that he could warn them as well of the danger that was present. He did not run away quietly, though. His feet made sucking and mucking sounds from being in the mud of the yard area between the house and the barn. It seemed to take forever for him to move even thirty feet.

The two parts of Ünger that were standing next to the second sentry looked up at the sound of Error running away. They rippled with hostility. Each beast was being disturbed from its prospective meal. This doubled part of Ünger saw the human moving away and sensed its fright. Panther and lizard alike smacked their lips together with anticipation and delight. Another fare was here for their ravenous glut to be sated. Not to be denied this new offering, the doubled demon split into two separate entities. The lizard section stayed near the hovering body. Moaning and hissing, it swayed from side to side. It prepared itself to deplete the remains of the corpse in front of it. The panther part yowled, shook itself and went after Error with a rancor and voracity not to be denied.

Savage watched the doubled part of Ünger unhinge itself into a panther and a lizard. The panther sprang after something it was watching; the lizard uncannily began to suck out the insides of the second corpse; and, the snake, with sheer ophidian efficiency, was completely immersed into draining away the remains of the initial sentry.

He could not keep staying in the barn. He had to get back outside and check on Pall. Surveying his location carefully once more, he initialized in his mind what he was going to do to get out of there. Once he had a plan of action to follow, the bowman decided to risk doing two things at once. He first emptied himself of all thought. Next, he softly walked to the front of the barn. Taking care that he absolutely made no sound, he prepared to escape from the barn's entrance. He gathered himself together and waited for a lightning strike, as his idea to get out of the barn unseen was to do so after one occurred. He hoped that the thunder that came afterwards would help cover any noise he might make in eluding the beasts.

At the point when a brilliant bolt of light sparked its way down into the nearby forest, Savage gathered himself together to leap out to the right side of the barn and then into the woods. He heard two of the patrols shouting at one another as they converged on the scene from opposite positions from where they were making their rounds on the perimeter of the farm.

Ünger—the snake and the lizard part of it—stopped their feeding. They looked up at the men running toward them and disengaged themselves from their victims. The men had half circled the two entities and were shooting arrows at the creatures to no avail. The missiles that were accurately aimed were just going through them without doing them any harm.

Several of the arrows went into the barn entrance, zipping by Savage as he folded himself against the inside wall of the entrance.

Forgetting the danger he was in, he observed the creatures as they sparkled, jittered to one another, disappeared and then reappeared in place again. In a particularly rapid set of glistening/unglistening, he watched as each one of them, the snake and the lizard, separately divided into two.

The sinister and foul things each created a new Ünger, Savage grimly noted to himself.

He wondered if these new beings could also divide into three more creatures. The information he had about Ünger did not take account of this dread cycle of multiplication.

How many times do these beasts recreate themselves? Does each have its own name; or, still go by the general term of Ünger?

Savage bleakly observed the four other worldly creatures that inhabited the yard and who now collectively stood looking flatly at the four Marauders in front of them.

The men confronting the demonic force about to attack them turned around and fled in absolute panic from the front of the barnyard.

Pall was in a state of pain beyond pain. His battle wounds and the burning sensation of the Valravn's blood coursed throughout him in flames of agony. The loss of feeling in his body, especially from being so tightly and cruelly bound for hours, did not help him either. Add the stress of being captured, and now about to be raped by Mustard, pushed him beyond the experience of having fevered hallucinations. He entered a place of fog, darkness and then absolutely nothing. He was in a vacuum where neither rational nor irrational thoughts were felt or processed. At first, when he entered this state, he became bemused watching himself observe his sense of awareness. He soon gave up this observation, mainly because he was exhausted. If it was possible to describe it, he would have said that he awoke into darkness and he forgot everything once more.

Mustard was upset. "What kind of fun can a man have when his boy is out of his senses," he complained to no one in particular. He had taken his pants off and was naked from the waist down.

Twin had tried to stop him, but the fat man had taken the hilt of the mercykiller and rapped Twin sharply on the side of the head several times with it. Then he had lifted Twin over his head and thrown him with great vigor into the opposite corner away from Pall. Although still somewhat conscious, Twin decided to stay where he was. He shook with anger, frustration and disgust at what the fat one was doing. Twin turned over on his other side and faced away from the other two men in the room. He curled into a fetal position.

Despite his anticipation in taking his way with Pall being disrupted and delayed, Mustard started to pleasure himself in front of the fire, away from where Pall lay huddled in the corner opposite Twin's. The fire in the hearth crackled. It spat sparks onto the floor in front of it. Rain fell on the thatched roof. He heard shouting and screaming outside the open window. Heaving a sigh of disgust that he could not proceed in having his bodily wishes met, he walked over to the window. Mustard still held himself without his knowledge of doing so. He peered with all his might into the darkness outside the farmhouse room.

A slight gust of wind tugged at the shutters and parted them open halfway. Another, pushed the left and right sides against the farmhouse wall.

Error had gone to the other twelve men who were sleeping in their temporary quarters. The green man had heard the shouts and warnings of the two patrols on the way to the row of sheds. He had also steeled himself to ignore their cries of alarm and terror. He awakened the sleeping Marauders, much to their annoyance at first. When he explained to them that they were under some kind of attack, they had gathered up their weapons and run out into the night. Some of them were angry at being brought out of a sound sleep. Some were petulant that Error was the cause of their being awakened so early. Others were curious about who had the temerity to be attacking them.

Error stopped them well before they reached the barnyard. He did not tell them what he had seen. He sent them in two waves of six men each. They were veterans of many pitched battles. They were best at close quarter infighting. Some of them enjoyed the exhilaration such combat brought them. Some took pride in their prowess and afterward would brag about and laugh with one another over such exploits. Others took a grim satisfaction at the fear they put in men's eyes, especially when the light of battle waned from them as they were being killed. He stayed behind to oversee their progress against their unknown opponents.

The panther that had taken off after the four men on patrol had run two of them down. It had placed both bodies together and proceeded to feed on them. The remaining two men fled away from one another in opposite directions. One took off into the woods. The other literally ran into Error. He had somewhat settled him down and sent him off to the farmhouse to warn Mordant what was happening to them.

The wind calmed down. The rain turned to a solid drizzle. The clouds overhead thinned out a little. The light of a full moon above them provided a dim, aqueous light to everything around the farm yard.

Savage could see other men approach the snake, the lizard and two Üngers. He also could see the shock of what they saw in front of them and he heard them call out warnings to one another. He gave them credit for their courage, foolish enough as it was in facing such a puissant terror arrayed before them in the night.

The snake and lizard grumbled something at the other Üngers. The call of a wood thrush filled the air around everyone present. Both parts of the first Ünger moved to either side of the two new creatures so that they were positioned between them. All four creatures started flowing toward the men. Savage watched in awe as the two Üngers each divided into three parts. Now eight beasts swarmed toward the humans opposing them.

In shock at what they were facing, and before common sense could take hold over them in what they were attempting to attack, the monsters were on them. Some of them fought valiantly to no avail. Some screamed in anger and abject terror. Others dropped their weapons and just blindly ran away. Most just died terribly and immediately.

Savage ran as well. However, he went out of the barn door entrance back to the farmhouse. Without seeing the bowman, the third patrol, with Mordant remaining behind, went past Savage. The men ran toward the sounds of panic ahead of them. Soon enough, their lamentation and death screams pushed the sound of the rain momentarily away.

Savage approached the back of the farmhouse. He saw a guard standing at the corner of the building trying to see what was causing the noise that was breaking out all over the barnyard area. Unaware of Savage's presence, his carelessness cost him his life.

The sentry stood stock still trying to decipher what was going on ahead of him.

The bowman silently approached him and slit the front of the sentry's throat in one deft stroke of his knife. Savage wiped the blade of his knife on the dead man's jerkin.

He heard another guard on his left call out to him, "Thomas, what is befalling us on the other side of the yard?"

Savage reached down to the man that he had so easily just dispatched and grabbed the man's helmet. He put it on his head. The helmet barely fit him. Making as if he were adjusting it to his head, he stooped down to the man's height and approached the other sentry. "I thought I heard something, too," he whispered softly.

The bowman had also taken the knife of the dead man from him. He now had two blades in each hand. The second guard walked right over to him after completely rounding the corner of the house. Savage sliced the man's left femoral artery with the knife in his right hand and drove the point of the other knife into the man's throat. He left it there in place. The guard dropped to the ground while giving a shocked gurgle of surprise. The big man placed the ill–fitting helmet silently on the ground besides the second guard's body.

Cries of battle in other parts of the farmstead filtered back to him. The rain drizzled to a stop. Savage took another turn around the side of the building then approached the front stealthily. He saw that the guards there, too, were trying to determine what was happening. He heard someone running toward them.

"What in the great God's name is going on out there?" asked one of them to the runner.

"We're under attack by monsters from hell," he shouted. "We need to get out of this cursed place now."

"Don't be foolish, man," one of the farmhouse sentries responded. "This lightning storm and evening have you unaccountably disturbed."

"You have no idea what has come upon us," the man panted at them as he stopped between them.

As the farmhouse sentry was about to respond to his breathless companion, Savage stepped in the middle of them. Shocked at his presence, they looked up at the seven foot giant looming in front of them. The panicked guard who was on perimeter patrol squeaked something inarticulate. He fell to the ground and started crawling away from them. One of the remaining sentries laughed at this display of cowardice. Savage took the pike being held by the one guard closest to him, held it mid quarters by the handle and drove the point of it into the man's chest. The point of the pike went through him and Savage pinned him against the wall of the house.

The remaining sentry exclaiming, "Hey, what are you doing: are you mad!"

The bowman did not verbally respond. Instead, he grabbed the other man by the neck with his right hand and chopped upward with the palm of his other hand into the man's nose. The force of the blow blew the bone into the other's brain, killing him instantly.

He walked over to the crawling man and placed his heel on the back of the man's neck. The man sobbed uncontrollably. "Who's in the house?" the bowman asked.

Nothing but piteous whimpering came out of him.

"I'm not going to ask you again. You best tell me who's in there."

"The Commander," came the barely discernible response.

"Who else?"

"I, I, don't know."

"Wrong answer," Savage said with contempt.

"A captive, I think," said the man abjectly; "along with Gordo," referring to Mustard.

"If I were in your position," the bowman advised, "I would get on my two good feet and retreat to a far safer space."

The man stood up. He was about to run back toward the barnyard. Savage grabbed him by the collar and spun him around. "The other direction, lad."

The man looked blankly at him.

"That way," Savage urged, and shoved him toward the other side of the building away from where he had been first running.

The man grunted in affirmation at this sound counsel. He ran away in the preferred direction Savage had just given him.

Error, seeing the disaster that was befalling his men, found the outhouse. Without any pretense of being proud, he smashed the seat in half and befouled himself into the excrement. Here he stayed throughout the remainder of the slaughter transpiring around him. To endure this suffering, he shut everything out of his mind.

Mordant, also seeing what was occurring, decided that discretion now ruled the disposition of his actions. He fled into the woods.

Mustard heard the struggle that was happening in the barnyard. He also heard what sounded like scuffling to him in the front yard of the farmhouse. He grabbed his pants with the thought that once they were on him, he could drag Pall out of the house and take him to another place where he could truly begin his ministrations with him. He put his pants on quickly then tried to secure the belt around his waist. Fumbling in his attempt to do so, he uttered imprecations against every known divinity in his spiritual landscape.

He heard a whooshing sound come through the window. Something stung him in the front of his stomach. He looked down at himself and recognized that a three foot arrow was embedded deeply into him with the point of it lodged against his spine. Blood started to leak slowly away from the entry point.

This is not right, he distantly thought. *I don't underst....*

The fat one sank to his knees. He could not stay on his feet. He was paralyzed.

Savage entered the room and took one look around it. A sword, embedded into the middle of the planked flooring eight feet in front of the hearth, was swaying slightly to and fro. For a brief moment, he thought it was a vertical eye blinking at him. He quickly shook that notion away from him and saw that the sheen of the blade was simply reflecting the light of the fire back at him. Yet, he could not dispel the thought that the sword was acting as a dispassionate eye witnessing the travesty that was unfolding in its midst.

The archer saw Pall motionless in one of the corners of the room on the floor. He also saw and heard Twin groan in the corner across the room from Pall. He checked the other remaining rooms, especially to locate the Commander. He found them all empty. Coming back into the main room, he went over to Pall and checked his condition more closely. Savage went back out of the house and grabbed clothing off of some of the men he killed on the way into the building. Back inside, he retrieved a worn blanket from one of the sleeping areas, and a knapsack filled with dried meat and fruit from the table in the kitchen.

Entering the main room again, he strode past a mewling Mustard, and went to Pall. He clothed him in shirt and pants and put the young man's boots back on his feet. Savage lifted Pall into his arms and walked across the room toward the door.

On his way past the fat man, he placed one of his feet on the lower part of the back of the man's neck. The bowman extended his leg forward in one quick movement. Mustard fell onto the floor with a loud grunt. Stomach first. Savage, with satisfaction, heard the arrow suitably snap in two underneath the craven man.

CHAPTER EIGHT

The light of the moon cast a sheen of white illumination over the area. Close by and far away, cries and screams could be heard. Men were being slaughtered in grotesque fashion.

Savage carried Pall out of the farmhouse. He brought him to the inside of a wattle fenced yard that was out of sight of anyone nearby. They were in one of the herb gardens, which was in close proximity to the house. It was nestled against the back wall of an ale making shed. In the waking hours, this space would have had the benefit of being in full sun throughout most of the day. The bowman gently placed Pall on the blanket that he earlier had taken from the farmhouse and put him in a sitting position against the back wall of the shed.

He knelt down beside the young man and asked, "Pall, can you hear me?"

There was no response. Not even a groan was uttered.

Savage placed the palm of his left hand to Pall's forehead.

"He's burning up," he commented to himself aloud.

At that moment, Twin appeared, carrying Pall's sheathed sword and his leather armor. He had discreetly started following Savage from the farmhouse from the moment the big man carried Pall outdoors. "He's in fairly rough shape," he said to the bowman when Twin was about ten feet away from him.

Savage looked at him. "Thanks to you and the part you and your companions had in making this lad's life more miserable than he deserves."

"Yes," admitted Twin, "I am responsible for being a party to his misery," he indicated in a sideways gesture with his right hand thumb toward the general direction of the farmhouse. "But I never wanted him to be treated the way he was, especially by Gordo," he added.

Savage gave a blank look at the name of Gordo.

"Gordo's the one you shot in the stomach," explained Twin.

"He deserved to be shot in the tail."

"I agree with you; it was warranted," said Twin. "And I am sure if you'd time, you would've sliced it off him."

"No," Savage stated flatly, "that *would've* been your job."

Twin's eyes opened wider than normal. "And, I would've done it without compunction or mercy."

Pall twitched violently and fell over to his side. Several grunts of pain were uttered.

Savage, with surprising gentleness, reached over to Pall's shoulders and again placed him against the wall of the ale shed.

At that moment, they heard a cricket chirp. Both men felt as though they were passing through cobwebs.

"Make your thoughts stop," Savage barely whispered to Twin. "Put your mind in a blank place," he cautioned.

"Who are you?" Pall asked as a man arising from the stream's depths, reached dry ground in front of him.

Or, *someone who looked like a man*, he thought as he saw that no water remained on him.

"I am Herald," was the response.

"Are you mortal?"

"Yes, if you like, but not in the sense that you know," Herald answered.

"What is happening to me, Herald?" Pall asked.

"I have been commissioned to appear before you in order to reveal to you what is imminent."

"What do you mean, Herald, am I not in a dream right now?"

"You may consider it a dream, but it is a harbinger to what is happening all around you."

"What are you here for, then?" Pall requested.

"This time is not what it seems. It is shrouded in darkness like a veil suspended before the stage of this world."

Neither understanding who Herald was, nor clear on what he was saying to him, Pall turned away from the strangeness of this other being. He looked at the massive black object on the water that was inexorably approaching them and inquired, "What is this dour object that approaches? The foreboding it gives off feels like death to me."

"You are correct in your knowledge of this foul thing," Herald said. "It is a negative force that impacts with life here in very harmful ways."

"Is it as appears to me a ship on the waters?"

Herald shrugged, "It appears differently to men exposed to its presence."

"I don't understand; am I dying?"

"Yes," Herald responded to Pall's question, "You have been in terrible straits and it has strained your body to its breaking point."

"Are you here to take me home?"

"No, Pall, I am not here for such purpose. This home, or heaven, is not yet available to you."

Herald put up his right hand toward the grim visage of the black ship. Pall could see a force of energy emerge from the being's hand. It reached the ship and covered it with light.

Pall blinked his eyes several times before exclaiming, "It is gone from here!"

Herald smiled gently at Pall. The being reached out to the young man and touched him gently on the forehead with his right index finger. He traced what seemed like a "T" on him. A strange sensation went through Pall. For some illogical reason, he opened his eyes.

Twin knelt before him in the moonlight. He saw Savage leaning against a wall immediately to his right. Both men appeared to have their eyes shut. They remained motionless and silent. Pall was not sure he was in a real place, but in another *dream*. It did not make sense for him to be where he was, especially with the reappearance of Savage and with Twin being in the bowman's company.

The clipped cadence of a wood thrush called out in the waning night.

The third, two-man patrol ran wildly by the ale shed. They had been late in arriving to the aid of their companions. Being the farthest away from the farmhouse, they had heard the sounds of horror being registered against the depredations of Ünger. But the sounds of this one–sided clash echoed strangely off the farmstead buildings and nearby forest. At first, they thought these shouts of dismay and terror were coming from the wagon road that passed the front entrance to the farm. Going through the woods in getting there proved futile in adding to their numbers against an unknown foe. They had run down the track into the farmstead proper and been caught up in the strange melee with Ünger.

Now, realizing firsthand what was happening, they fled by the three men in the wattle fenced in yard.

Pall thought he saw a flickering shape like a panther, or some kind of leopard, detach itself from the far end of the fence. It paused, and after looking at the fleeing men for a moment, turned its full gaze toward Pall. He felt the eyes connect with his like a shock. It was as though he had been lit up from inside. His whole body started to heave in a violent shudder.

Yet, despite this appalling feeling, something like hope overcame him. Deep within Pall's awareness a song came to him. He had never heard it sung before, but when he listened to it building within his mind, he felt that it was an ancient plea for help. He closed his eyes. He saw Herald smiling at him. Pall opened his heart to the song and sang:

> Sorrow and Sickness ever follow me.
> Wrath and Humiliation descend
> without cease.

Even though the light of day
Suffuses me with its beauty and
Surrounds me
with its saffron urgency—
Though the still of the night
closes my eyes—
I stand as a cipher of pain:
A stalk of wild rye
Swaying in the winds
of anger.
A sojourner,
As all my fathers before me;
With no ground that is home under my feet,
As a pilgrim ceaseless in my wandering,
I yet hold on to the
Torment of birth,
As mothers even now are loath
to deliver an undesired child.
O,
Angel of Mercy,
To what shrine do I now bow before
to rid me of these pangs?
Let me not cling
to such vaunted
Distress.
Open a heart turned to stone.
I look to you Lord
for your grace and goodness

to shine down upon me.
Let neither my iniquity swallow
My soul,
Nor my sin worship
A vain mistress.
Deliver me from the oppression of my enemies.
Guide my feet to walk in your ways and
onto the path to your throne.

The panther part of Ünger bleakly eyed the singing being in front of it. It responded in distaste upon hearing the song uttered in its presence. Yet, even though the melody and words sent a signal through Ünger to avoid it and get away from its sound, it nevertheless took several long strides toward the young human before him. It was fascinated by him, and took faint notice of the other two men nearby Pall. It sniffed the air greedily trying to savor the mortal's human signature. It paused. The great beast shook its head with agitation. Slaver spilled over its lips and spooled in loops toward the ground. The spatter of it on the grass in front of the fence caused it to foam and boil. It was as if the grass had been thrown into a hot cauldron and was being sautéed in preparation of a greater meal about to be made.

It closed its eyes. It weaved back and forth to the song's rhythms. It went completely still. Its tail dropped to the ground.

Savage and Twin, hearing the song being voiced had opened their eyes. With great concern and expecting the beast to launch itself immediately upon them, they were yet affixed into place. Twin shook as though the worst ague in his life assaulted him. Savage yearned to nock an arrow to his great bow. They could not move, neither to flee nor to fight the translucent menace before them.

They watched the panther close its eyes. They heard it grumble as though vocal cords long unused to making such sounds were trying to force an utterance. It slowly began to croon along roughly with Pall's singing. It did not sing but sounded as a giant insect in the midst of its stridulating.

A large sinuous shape snaked by the panther in full glide toward the quickly disappearing patrol. It swiped the panther almost off its feet as it flickered by it. This time the beast stopped its discord. It opened its eyes.

Savage could have sworn that the apparition at this moment almost smiled.

The beast turned quickly about and silently leapt after the patrol.

CHAPTER NINE

Pall finished the song. He slumped back against the wall spent with a sense of loss over what he knew not.

Savage shook himself from the torpor in which he had been held.

Twin continued to shudder.

"I didn't know what you were doing, lad, when you started your song," Savage said as he knelt once again by Pall's side. "I thought you were in shock and gone daft."

Twin nodded, or at least appeared to be as his shaking began to get under control.

"I didn't know I was going to do that—to sing, I mean," Pall said, "It just, came to me all of a sudden."

Savage looked at Pall with grave concern.

They remained silent for a moment. Screams filled the air around them from different locations nearby.

"The young master looks spent," exclaimed Twin softly. "Yes, I imagine that's the least he's feeling," agreed Savage. "What's going on, Savage? What is happening to us? Why are you with Second," Pall inquired.

"They call me Twin, although the name's more insult than not," responded Twin.

Savage shook his head with an accompanying wave of negation at the man. The bowman quickly shared with Pall what had transpired since they last saw one another.

Twin filled in what Savage did not know.

"It's time you moved away from here," Savage whispered to Pall.

"To where?"

"You are going to use the field we came in to this place to leave here."

Pall looked doubtfully at the big man.

"Skirt the fields at the edge of the woods and then head out onto the road Twin and his band of Marauders used. Twin will help you, won't you Twin," Savage stated as a command rather than a question.

This time, Twin nodded perceptibly and said, "Yes, I'll help him. It's the least I can do to assuage the blame on me for helping hurt him."

"Aren't you going with us, Savage?" Pall asked.

"Not at the moment, Pall. I have things I must do first."

"Once we get on the road, if we make it alive that far, where do we head for?"

"There's another farm, an even bigger one two miles back where we came from on the wagon road," Twin offered.

"No!" Savage exclaimed immediately. "Stay away from any dwelling place. They're likely to have been all corrupted."

Twin looked down at the ground shamefaced. "We pretty much laid waste to a lot of people and their belongings."

"Never mind that, Twin. Help Pall. Get going now!"

"Will I see you again, Savage? Pall asked.

"Yes, you will," assured the big man. "But, how will you find us?"

"Go in the direction the Marauders were first going. Ford through two streams. The second large field you get to, stop there. Stay inside the woods. There are thickets of alder and hickory near the edge of the tree line. Wait for me there for a half day. If by noon you haven't seen me, continue walking on the road. I'll find you."

"Pall smiled, "Wow!" he said with a faint smile on his face. "That's quite a mouthful you just delivered."

The bowman briefly placed his hand onto Pall's shoulder and said, "Yes, quite a peroration for the likes of me."

Twin solicitously helped Pall to stand.

Pall almost slapped Twin's hands away. He was not used to the man being friendly. Yet, he restrained himself from doing so. He knew he needed his help.

Twin made to give Pall his sword back.

Pall shook his head, saying, "No you hold onto it for now."

He saw that his leather armor was also draped over Twin's left arm. Pall silently accepted his armored clothing. He sat down, took his boots off and then stood up to put on the shirt and pants that his stepmother and father had so lovingly made for him. Once on, he stepped into his boots and tied the leather laces securely on each one of them. His hands automatically searched for knives on his belt that were no longer available to him.

Savage picked up the blanket Pall had been sitting on. He folded it loosely lengthwise and handed it to Twin. He then offered him the pack of food. "Step lively now: Go...." he directed.

Twin took the proffered cloth and draped it around his neck, while he slung the leather strap to the pack across one of his shoulders. "What happens if those beasts come upon us again?" he asked Savage.

The big man looked at Pall and said, "The lad's spent. I don't think he's got another enchantment or prayer in him to ward off Ünger and its divisions. Do what I first told you to do when you sense the creatures are near you."

Twin looked very doubtful at this information.

"It's the best I can tell you both. Stay out of their sight. Go still. Empty yourself of thought."

All three moved through the ale house's herb garden and left the wattle fenced in area.

Pall and Twin went toward the field Savage and Pall had first entered into the farmstead.

Savage went back along the sheds where Mordant's men had slept, roughly paralleling the barn's location.

No clouds remained overhead. The moon rode silently and all alone in the nighttime sky. Its brightness diffused the light of any other stars. There was no wind. No sound came from any creature except the remaining few who were still alive and trying to bolt away from further harm due to Ünger's greed for mortal flesh.

Pall and Twin found themselves in the same expanse where the blacksmith's son and Savage first approached the farmhouse the evening before. Nothing untimely halted their progress back down the fallow field. They stayed to the right of the field alongside the drip edge of the trees bordering the cleared ground. Within a minute they were soaking wet.

Twin blurted out the statement, "Cursed rain!"

Then he added, "Cursed place! Cursed time! Cursed moon! Cursed...."

"Pray be silent with your profanity, Twin," Pall exhorted him with a whispered warning. "You'll bring further wrath upon yourself and me."

Twin snorted at this admonishment. "There's nothing but evil around us," he snorted. "What else but darkness and ill will have descended upon us."

"True," Pall agreed with the glum sounding man reluctantly. "However, we have escaped so far from a vicious enemy. And, once you were one of my captors, yet here you are helping deliver me from the ship of death."

They had reached the end of the field. They stopped momentarily to assess the gloom of the forest proper.

"Only hours ago," Pall said, "I thought these woods were under the blessings of a caring guardian. I don't get that feeling so much now."

Twin remained silent.

"Savage wanted us to go inside the edge of the tree line and follow it back out through the farm toward the track you came in on," the young man said.

Twin maintained his silence. He appeared to be listening to something Pall did not apprehend.

"Twin, what's going on with you?"

"I thought I heard something."

"When, right now?"

"Yes," came the reply. "I heard something else earlier, too. When we were approaching where we're now standing."

Pall listened with all of his senses tuned to detecting any ill–starred sound. Hearing nothing, he urged Twin to follow Savage's directions.

"Right now," Twin said, "I am afraid to move. Suppose it's that demon thing. We should get farther into the woods and put our thoughts aside."

"I can't do that, Twin. We'll never get out of here if we start doing that over every sound we think we've heard."

"Very well. Very well. All right—let's just get going along here," he pointed deeper into the forest.

Without further ado about their fears of being brought once again into battle with Ünger, they plunged a greater distance into the trees. They could see the field they had just traversed lit up under the moon's splendor. Everything in the distance under its touch appeared as if made by the hand of a protean silversmith. It had a strength to it that was unworldly. The common appearance of nature had a sublime, even cherished, polish to it. Had both men the time, they would have stood in wonder at the sight of the spectacle before their eyes.

The clamor from the killing spree Ünger had unleashed throughout the farmstead had all but ceased. Occasionally, they heard a muted cry. This sound of mortal strife soon ended. All that could be heard was the water dripping down upon and around them in the wood.

They could see through the trees that another field intersected with the one they were following. Brightness illuminated farmland on their left and ahead of them. They slowly approached the edge of this new opening.

Reaching the verge of the expanse before them, Twin whispered, "It would be foolish to go across the middle."

Pall nodded in agreement to this assertion.

Twin said, "Let's follow this farmland on its edge and turn along with it."

Again, Pall agreed silently, but indicated with a nod of his head for Twin to set the lead. Pall felt dizzy. He started to sway back and forth.

Twin reached out to Pall and steadied the young man from falling down.

Twin set Pall's sword that he was carrying against the trunk of a tree. He reached into the pack slung across his shoulder that Savage had given him earlier in the yard of the ale shed. "Here," he offered Pall whatever he had quickly grabbed from the pack. "I think you better eat something. I know I could use some nourishment as well."

Pall took the kind offering of food. He could not remember when he had last eaten. "Thank you, Twin," he said graciously.

They stood in place for a brief moment of time while they ate their food.

As they started to walk back into the recesses of the forest, Twin quickly signaled silence. "I heard something again," he said nervously.

"You're overwrought, Twin."

"No, this time I definitely heard a noise."

"Well, what does it sound like?"

"Someone's coming, or following us. I heard footsteps moving quickly toward our position."

Pall once again attempted to assay the truth of Twin's insistence that someone, or something, was soon to be upon them. Hearing and feeling nothing sinister or another's presence, he shook his head back and forth, saying, "Let's keep moving and see if it follows us."

Again, they walked as stealthily as they could summon the strength to do so along another field within a healthy depth of the woods. Reaching the end of this field's length, they now followed its course away towards the left.

The uncommon, preternatural silence continued. They came to the end of the section of the field whose border they were tracking.

An additional section was reached until they had passed three fields in total.

"I think we are on the side of the last field before the wagon track," Twin said thoughtfully. "From what I recall in entering this farm from the other side, this field angles down off to the left."

"Okay, let's get to the wagon track," Pall urged. "We need to keep staying out of plain sight."

They followed the traverse line of the border between forest and field until they were two-thirds of the way to the public roadway.

"I need to stop!" Twin said with strangled vehemence. Pall looked inquiringly at the other fellow.

"I just know someone's following us."

Paul asked with some doubt, "How can you be so certain?"

"Because I have the gift of knowing when such a thing occurs."

"Good, "Pall averred. "Then we know that it's not a beast that stalks us, but man instead. Let's just continue getting to the road."

Hedges started to impede their progress. They walked more toward the open land next to them. Doing so increased their speed, shortening the time they had left in getting to the wagon track. Soon, they almost spilled into the beaten down pathway, which truly was only a somewhat rough track through large tracts of uninhabited land.

They held back underneath the shadows of the tree line.

"Let me get my bearings here," Twin said.

He poked his body out further from the trees to look up and down the roadway. "Savage wants us to go this way," he indicated to the right. "Not the way those Marauders approached the farm."

"Should we walk here in the road?" asked Pall.

"May as well. I think we're beyond the immediate ken of the monster. Besides, it's too busy cleaning up its dinner for the likes of us."

They proceeded quickly down the path for which they had so previously yearned.

Walking in a gradual downhill line for another half mile or so, they came to an intersection. They could see by the contours of the other path that it was less used as the one they were presently on.

Twin expressed his concern about their staying on the main path. "I think Savage wanted us to take this one," indicating the lesser traveled lane.

"I don't think that was part of his directions to us," Pall said doubtfully.

An argument broke out between them over what Savage's travel advice was given to them. Soon enough, it became heated. As the debate began to cross over into injurious territory of insult traded for insult, a loud noise of something crashing through the woods on the right was heard approaching them with unalterable speed.

Twin looked at Pall.

"Sure, sure. Sure. Repeatedly so. You were right," Pall said. "Even I hear that."

The *that* Pall heard exploded into their presence and fell down prostrate in the road before them. He was almost without apparel on due to his clothes being in tatters. In first looking at him, the rips, rents and tears were so extensive on him that it was difficult to determine where in places the clothes ended and the body began, or even where in places the body began and the clothes ended.

For some reason he could not yet fathom, the man in front of him on the ground looked familiar to

Pall. He could not place him until Twin said affably, "Hello, Twin! I see you have been exerting yourself prodigiously so."

The man addressed as the second Twin put up his hands and tried to speak. The deep draughts of air that he was attempting to take in prevented him from saying anything coherent.

Pall looked back and forth at both of them trying to determine if he were hearing things. *The first Twin called a greeting to the second one*, he thought. All of a sudden, it dawned on him, *This is First and Second. They're twins with the same name!*

Second asked First for an explanation about how First had arrived in front of them.

First again attempted to express himself, but the result was the same as the first time.

"Let him catch his breath," Pall said. "Let me catch a break here because my head's spinning trying to figure out who's who between the two of you."

"We don't have time for him to dawdle here in the open road, and at a crossways, too," Second stated.

"Give him a brief respite to do so anyway," Pall responded. "Why," he added, "do you both have the same name?"

"We don't have the same name. Well, we have the same last name but not our first names."

"Well, go on, tell me more," Pall urged the man on to explain this mystery.

"When we joined up with the Marauders, no one could tell us apart. They kept getting us confused with one another. So to keep it simple for them, Captain Error told everyone to call us each, Twin."

Pall laughed and asked, "What are your real first names?"

Second responded saying, "My name is Merek."

An out–of–breath squeak from First could barely be understood except for the phrase, "My name is Carac."

"Fine," Pall said, and turning to Second addressed him with some irony, "It is an honor to meet you Merek."

Turning back to First, he extended his hand outward towards him. First grasped Pall's right forearm. Pall did likewise and as he was helping him to his feet he said, "And it is an honor to meet you Carac."

"Although," Pall added to the two men before him, "you did not start off very honorably in the beginning meeting me."

The twins apologized as profusely as they were able to Pall, particularly under the circumstances in which they found themselves. Carac, like his brother Merek, felt obligated to help Pall. As Savage did earlier, the twins caught up with one another and with Pall as well, on what had happened to each of them since they had last been together.

It was Carac who had been sent away to get help from the initial barnyard massacre that Savage had also viewed. Unseen by Error, and in a temporary place of hiding from the monsters, Carac watched the shaken Captain run past him toward the privy.

Dodging actively hunting phantom panthers, lizards and snakes, Carac worked his way toward the woods past the ale shed.

"I heard someone singing a very haunting song, and what sounded at the same time as growling," he said.

Merek explained, "You heard the lad here pourin his heart out at one of the beasts."

Carac gave his account of what happened when he was at the ale shed. "I was on the other side of it opposite where the panther beast appeared. I couldn't see what was goin on because I was so filled with terror. I couldn't move."

"Neither could Savage and me," Merek added soothingly. Pall stopped listening so attentively to the twins' conversation. He thought he had heard something coming from the woods through which Carac had fled into the open road.

Carac continued his narrative, "After the growlin I was able to stand up, but I still couldn't move away from there. When the singin ended, I fled into the woods without bein stopped by any demonic looking creature."

"Was it you who was following us?" Merek asked of his brother.

"Aye," Carac replied, "but I was tryin me best to be quiet, especially with the hearin you have, brother, for scoutin such that be followin you."

"Now stop talkin in the accent our Da used to use for fun with us."

"I can't help meself, Merek. I'm nervous and scared beyond my wits."

"Why, Carac, what's put you into such an agitated state?"

"Because I sensed somethin' followin me. Somethin," he emphasized carefully, "that made me feel as though spiders were crawlin over my body, especially after I had been in the woods trying to catch up with you."

Merek had taken a deep breath but did not dispel any air as he listened to his brother alarm him with this news.

"Then I heard a cricket creak out a very odd sound for a cricket. It started makin me feel like I was goin through spider webs. I ran away from followin you and fled along the edge of the fields. The things were glidin after me, laughin and droolin at my fear. I got tangled up and bloody in briars. Fortune saw to it that I ran onto the road almost on top of you."

The Twins looked at Pall as he started to run away from them.

Merek was next to run in the same direction Pall took. When Pall was more than two hundred feet away, a bird song could be clearly heard in the woods above the Twins' heads. It was the interrupted call of a wood thrush.

CHAPTER TEN

Boiling out of the forest came the three dreadful divisions of the third Ünger. They swarmed over Carac.

Pall stood transfixed as they growled, chittered and hissed in glee at their freshly acquired prize.

Merek caught up to Pall. He quickly dropped the blanket around Pall's neck and transferred the falchion sword and the scabbard that he had been carrying to its rightful owner. He then promptly placed the leather strap of the food pack over Pall's shoulder as well. "Run!" he urged.

Both men ran down opposite sides of the lesser traveled path.

Merek went to the right. Pall to the left.

A last cry shuddered out of Carac's throat and followed after the fleeing men. It seemed to descend upon their fast retreating forms as in a haunting of a terrible, inevitable infliction of death. "Oh, brother, why doesn't the boy sing his prayer for...."

Without recognizing it, tears were freely falling from Pall's eyes as he ran from the wretched scene. Being overwhelmed by Ünger's unholy trinity once more felt as though its earlier plague of ill–omened predation now reached an unthinkable level of vengeance. Its earlier spree of violence was just a prelude to a final burst of murder, This time, the mere sight of them alone burned his entire cognizance away. The young man's consciousness became an empty vessel.

He was neither aware of the direction in which his rapidly moving feet went, nor how much distance they put him away from the scene of Carac's demise. Considering what he had recalled going through since he arose from the field of battle, he could not understand how his body could find the strength to reach such an elusively sought safety.

Eventually, he found that he could no longer see the path on which he had been following.

The moon had completely waned.

It was solid darkness before the dawn.

He walked slowly now. Carefully, he stepped into the company of the trees around him. He could feel their presence as he passed by a score or more of them.

I hope they're copper beeches, he thought.

Pall had played out any reserves of strength that he had. He leaned his scabbarded sword against the wide bole of one of the elder trees.

He finally stretched himself out on the ground in the predawn hour of the night. He was tired beyond his capacity to care about putting the threadbare blanket that Savage had found, and which was eventually given to him by Merek, around him or onto the ground. The night was enough for him. He wrapped the evening around him darkly. Appropriate for his mood.

After a long time of being unable to sleep, he rose and went to sit underneath another, even larger tree than before. The blacksmith's son wedged himself in between the large roots emanating from the base of the tree trunk. He set his back to the tree and shrugged himself comfortably into the smooth, barked pattern of its ridge print. Thinking beyond the memory of the day before, his mind was cast into a silent reverie from his past; and yet, he slept, nevertheless, and fully at last.

CHAPTER ELEVEN

He was eighteen. His father had fashioned for him a simple but effective "suit" of armor. The shirt had been made from specially cured and hardened leather. It was wrapped over individual plates of thinly hardened steel. Supple and lightweight, it had been shaped into ovals, circles and roundels, which were cleverly stitched together with wound silk, jute and horsehair. Protective pieces in the lower front and back could be attached as well to protect the respective parts of his body that would ordinarily be exposed to the degradation of hand weapons and arrows. His pants had a similar theme of protection. Also lightweight, they offered him a welcome freedom of movement and defensive covering. His mother had made linen undergarments over which he could comfortably wear this suit.

Boots were made for him by the local shoemaker. The leather used for them was made in two parts. The inner face of the footwear was made from unusually soft pieces of calfskin. It easily conformed to the shape of his feet, ankles and reached the mid-calf of his leg. The outside of the boots were reinforced with hardened leather. Compacted together with specially made glue for such a purpose, they also were given a unique treatment of oils on the outside surface that made them virtually waterproof. The complete outfit amounted to an additional, and invaluable, weapon.

Yet, the miracle of blacksmithing had been surpassed with the forging of his sword and set of fighting knives. It had taken his father months of designing, and consulting with other veterans in the village and surrounding countryside, as well as with the professional fighters and warriors visiting him for purchase of their own hand made weapons. To make these weapons for his son, Blacksmith Warren arose earlier in the morning than his normal routine allowed. He also spent extra time after his day's business at the forge and anvil were done working to complete his son's fighting weapons. Three separate sets of weapons were made and found not to the craftsman's exact standards. These attempts were melted down once again after being tested in their degree of efficacy in defensive and offensive moves.

The fourth time Warren stepped to the making of steel for his son came after a lapse of six months. During this time, he experimented with different samples of iron and alloyed steel. He again consulted the other blacksmiths in the region whom he respected and asked for their advice on the best raw materials that could be found for his purposes.

A great warrior had arrived one day at Warren's forge seeking the master smith's help in making new weapons for him. To the blacksmith's delight, the warrior had also brought his own metal with him that had been obtained from a far land thousands of miles from this part of their world. Its ductility, strength and capability in being refolded and quenched multiple times were something the smith had never witnessed before in his experience as a warrior and as a master craftsman. He struck a deal with the champion before him and made the warrior's weapons free for the price of obtaining enough of the iron he had brought with him for the making of his son's sword and fighting knives.

Pall remembered the day when his father and mother presented him with the clothes and weapons that were made for him with such mastery, strength and love. Father, mother and son fasted, prayed and then celebrated this solemn, yet thrilling, moment. Every part and process in procuring and making the clothes and boots were accompanied with singing, blessings and prayers. The cycle of forging and working with the rare metal to be incorporated into Pall's clothes for his hand weapons was given equal, if not even more, exalted attention. Often, more than not, the blacksmith would spend all night working on them. Despite these long and arduous hours, Pall and his mother would find David in the morning full of vitality and smiling at them.

"You should see what this metal can do!" he would frequently tell them. Referring to its properties he would also exclaim, "It's uncanny how it works with me. I think there's a part of me that recognizes it's a living substance with its own intelligence and awareness. I think sometimes in the night when I am working *with* it, that it is fashioning me and not the other way around."

He paused in mid–thought, then added, "We sing together when the hammering occurs. I share with it the battles and encounters I have had in my own days of warfare and command."

Realizing that he had been talking to his family in superlatives and in mystery, he stopped himself from saying anything else further, and smiled sheepishly at them. Pall wanted to ask his father more questions regarding what the blacksmith was referring to in being with the metal. If his mother were present at such moments, she would look at her son, shake her head demurely and try to change the subject. When he was alone with his father and hearing such praise and wonder about the metal, especially what it brought out in his memory, he would begin to ask his father to say more about what he meant. But he could never get these questions answered. The older man would get a faraway look on his face, become quiet and lapse into a deep mood of contemplation. Out of respect for his dad, Pall would get similarly quiet and still.

Pall had been studying and sparring with his father since Pall could walk and carry a practice sword and set of knives. The blacksmith would make time to teach his son the art and science of close quarter combat and practice with him as well. The smith could see that while his son was admirably adept at a wide variety of weapons, he was gifted at hand–to–hand fighting. However, when it came to using the sword, quarterstaff and knives, Pall entered the realm of a rare and superlative form of combat.

Recognizing his son's genius at doing so, the smith would find occasions when the warriors visiting the forge for their armor and weapons to be custom made were also willing to practice fight with his son as the boy began maturing into a young man. The smith cautioned the boy never to embarrass these men by defeating them at their practice bouts.

"You can come close," Warren would smile at his son, "but keep them confident and on the offense against you."

"Why, Da?" the boy once asked.

"Because," came the elder Warren's laconic response, "It gives you more practice: more practice gives greater endurance and the freeing of thought in a sustained attack."

The boy thought a bit more about what his father stated to him and then looked inquiringly at his dad for more information.

The smith smiled gently at the boy, saying, "It also makes them feel more generous towards teaching you and paying me the money they owe us."

Father and son broke into laughter.

Pall shifted his position under the copper beech. He opened his eyes and saw that it was just about dawn. A soothing dim light began filling the early morning sky. Pall could make out that he was in the middle of a stand of at least a dozen or more Sentinel Trees. Closing his eyes once again, he moved onto his right side using his upper right arm as a pillow for his head. He soon fell back into a restless, but deep, sleep.

"Pray, Pall, pass the ale down this way," the blacksmith said.

He turned to his wife and stated with a full smile on his expression, "And, Lucia, kindly send the wine over to me so I may pour its beauty into three of these four cups before me."

Pall grinned and stood up from the table. On a side table next to him were arrayed four empty goblets and a pitcher of ale. He poured a goblet's full of ale for his father, and then one equally as generous for his mother. First serving his mother with a flourish of his now empty left hand, he walked over to his father and saluted him sharply. Pall returned to his seat and set himself in it before a well–made, sturdy table, filled with an ample, but simple, celebration fare.

The elder Warren poured a deep red colored wine into three cups. He took everything in before him with an appreciative look and nodded approvingly. Glancing at his wife and son, he looked last at a fourth table setting and chair, which was placed to his immediate right.

"At the end of this well prepared repast, Pall, you will exchange the seat you are now in for this one," he said with a slight smile now on his face.

Pall nodded at his father. His father and mother had told him how this supper was going to unfold in detail the evening before.

"There will be two toasts during our time here together: One, will be taken by you in the place where you presently sit—for you are seated here as you have ever been placed at our table and since you could do so upright in a chair with us. The other, will be taken by you here in the honored guest's chair. Here before those who love you the most deeply in this current

117

realm, you will transform yourself from the well tread path of youth to the initial journey of a soldier."

The blacksmith served his wife first. He poured a cup for Lucia and walked it over to her. After setting the cup next to her right hand, he bent slightly to her and kissed her gently on the forehead. He walked back to his place at the head of the table. Warren poured a cup for himself and one for his son. Walking over to Pall, he set the cup before the young man in the same place as he had done so for Lucia. He kissed his son lightly on the top of his head, something the blacksmith had not done since Pall could recall.

Lucia bowed her head and said in strong, humble tones, "Blessed be this table, food and wanderers before it. Grace be upon us and a special honor placed upon my husband David as he calls down the blessings of the Lord in the manner of countless generations of fathers before in our family."

The blacksmith smiled again. He looked steadily at the two individuals before him, saying, "We come before the throne of the God of families. We ask that mercy and grace rain down upon us; that the strength of love and peace embrace our hearts; and, that the food presented before us be a blessing to our spirits. We thank you for the son you have given us. We commit him to your will and we place his feet upon your ways."

With the foregoing prayer given, all three Warrens drank as one.

Pall remembered how much he strove to keep every detail of this time in his memory. Yet, he yearned to get to the receiving of the gifts his mother and father had made and obtained for him. The meal was delicious. There was much laughter. Memories, precious, mundane, and most of all cherished, were shared together.

How can almost twenty years pass so quickly by? Pall asked himself at one point toward the end of their meal with one another.

Soon, the food had all but been eaten. The ale and wine quaffed.

A reverent silence overtook them into their own private and collective memories.

Mother, father and son shook the moment of quiet off their silent meditations. They arose from the table, clearing all the remnants of the food and the three settings away into the kitchen area.

Returning to the table, Lucia and David stood respectively to the left and right of the fourth chair.

Pall entered into the room and approached them. Lucia pulled the chair away from the table for her son. She bade him to be seated in it, to which Pall gracefully did so. She returned to her own revered chair and stood behind it.

119

Seeing his wife ready to be seated, he helped slide Pall's chair closer to the table's edge. The master smith walked to his chair. He stood behind his chair and bade his wife to be seated.

David pulled his chair out, but he remained on his feet before the table. He poured the red wine into and almost to the top of the fourth cup. Pall stood up from his chair. His father served his son first, immediately taking his right forearm with his right hand clasped in an ancient warrior's greeting of friendship and brotherhood.

Taking his powerful right hand in an upwards sweep, he used it to hit a restrained, downward strike with the bottom of his clenched fist just above Pall's heart.

Initially referring to himself, Warren said, "May the power and wisdom of this man's arm be transferred to the heart and arms of the man receiving it."

"So be it said," the former commander intoned.

"So be it finished," the emerging warrior before him concluded.

CHAPTER TWELVE

He again awoke underneath the Sentinel Tree. It was full light. Sunlight, birdsong and a soft breeze saturated the air around the old copper beech and the human who had sought shelter under its canopy. He soaked these sounds into him as if he were a thirsty man who now had a liberal source of water to revive his body and spirits. He listened with an almost avid attention to his environment. Pall did not discern any human sounds. He relaxed somewhat and took a deep breath of fresh forest air into him.

Pall stood up onto his feet. He felt a flow of former memories cascading into his thoughts. He held them off, saying aloud, "Let me get my bearings in the daytime. I'll just take a bit of time to break my fast, eat something from the pack Merek gave me "

Upon mentioning Second's real name to himself, full remembrance of the previous night and day returned to him with stunning impact. He summoned a prayer within his spirit and sent it to the Heavens above as a petition of peace, blessing and thanks for helping him survive.

He ate sparingly from the hastily obtained provisions in the pack. When he was finished eating, Pall walked over to where he had placed his sword and scabbard against the trunk of the great tree.

Picking up the gift his father had made for him, he drew the sword from the hand tooled scabbard that his mother and father both made for him. He put the scabbard down on the ground next to the bole of the Sentinel in front of him.

He saw Error again in the farmhouse, taking the sword in the green man's hand and coveting it for its deadly beauty as he whipsawed the blade perilously close to him.

Sunlight dappled on him and the sword he held. He carefully examined it. Again, Pall was astonished at the weapon's light weight and how it felt so comfortably in his right hand. His muscles, ligaments, tendons and bones seemed to cry a welcome to its familiarity.

Deep within the memory of his heart, Pall heard his father talk to him: "This is a two–edged, falchion sword, an offensive weapon that can be wielded with one or two hands. It is a living image of a blade borne by an ancient prince of long ago, whose deities blessed his being a blazing beacon of war in battle. When done so with mastery, a great power can be unleashed for combat. You have but to meld in a complete courtship with it. The blade knows not defeat. It seeks victory through the strength and knowing of the person wielding it."

For a moment, the full light of the sun reflected off the part of the blade near the hilt grasped easily in his hand. The flashing light blinded him to his present whereabouts and carried memories of his past into him like a rushing current of the ocean's tide.

They had finished their training for the day. As it was towards the end of their initial phase in being new recruits in the King's army, they were given an early evening's leave to find their own meal and entertainment. Nine of them decided to go to one of the taverns in the town nearby that was known by the soldiers to welcome them sincerely into its noisy and boisterous confines. As per their sergeant's orders and army regulations, they were without their arms, especially so as they would be mingling with civilians and other soldiers from other units and commands.

With so much male competition existing between rival factions of the army and the hypervigilance everyone kept in order to maintain combat readiness, altercations were not only common, but eagerly sought. Tempers, patience and pride seemed to soar when liquor, drink and women were involved with one another. Also, when bravado, unit pride and young fighters were in close proximity to one another, it was inevitable, a law of nature that collisions occurred between and among them.

Flush with being paid their wages for the last fortnight, these nine young fighters could afford the higher prices of this tavern than its nearby competitors. For an additional price they could seat themselves closer to the hearth where its warmth in the late autumn, along with the victuals and ale of the tavern keeper, were more immediate and better in quality than elsewhere in the tavern.

The nine young men eagerly entered into the tavern's main door, elbowing one another laughingly out of the way. Arriving at the mutually agreed upon table near the fire, they discovered that another group, composed of eleven veterans, had their collective eye on the same spot. The two groups of men approached the table at the same time from opposite sides of one another.

The spokesman for the larger group was a grizzled warrior of thirty–three years of age. Tall, lean and muscular, he had a commanding presence about him. His companions, nine of whom were of equal severity, age and experience, deferred to him in stoic silence. The eleventh companion was slightly older than his peers. He was a giant of a man. The other men favored him with their respect and wariness.

"I see we have some young chickens here who wish to roost on our spot," the spokesman for the veterans said in a matter–of–fact tone.

The spokesman for the nine recruits was the youngest and wealthiest of them all. It was not just money that made him thus. He had a brash grace, a too quick tongue and a glibness of speech that could charm a dress off a young woman before she was conscious of being so pliant to him.

"Your honor has a keen eye for fresh fowl, yet cries foul freshly," he quipped.

Men at nearby tables began to go quiet. They could sense something auspicious, especially in terms of entertainment, about to begin between these two opposing groups of men in their midst.

Upon hearing the jibe of the young man, the elder warrior retorted with a longstanding understatement to the junior version of himself who was attempting to oppose him over table rights. "While you seem clever to you and your young progeny, my young hen, you charm no one but yourself. Move away now while your wings remain unclipped by the fowlers' daggers."

His opposite uncurled a wicked smile, and with a twinkle in his eyes challenged, "No wings by foul methods will be clipped on this side of the table; but I wager good money daggers of this fowl will ensnare your own."

A couple of the veterans around their leader, snorted derisively, but kept their peace.

Several customers nearby lightly applauded the brashness and wit of the young man.

"Well, hen," menacingly responded the veteran, "What exactly do you propose to bet on that will easily see you bested by your superiors?"

"As our arms are in our quarters in camp, I propose we use those the good God gave us to settle the matter. Winner takes the table. Loser serves the winner ale and supper."

Quietly, several men farther away from the now central action in the room began to bet on which group of men on either side of the table would win in a soon to be defined match by the contestants themselves.

"Speak plainly now, pigeon, you fly in dangerous territory."

"Yes, yes," the young recruit said with slight contempt in his manner. "Age such as you and yours have accrued comes with the attendant infirmities of mixed metaphors and mixed notions filled with false pride."

Most of the room was now quiet. Only the servers could be heard moving from table to table. Soon, though, even they became still and began watching for the outcome of this particular brawl in the making. The betting slowly increased in the number of willing participants eager to do so.

"Careful, boy, tread lightly, and we will still be gentle in breaking your bollocks. What feat of our arms do you wish to engage in?"

"Lads," crowed the younger one of the two spokesmen, "we've been given a battle promotion from being birds to humans. Looks like we're starting to win already!"

The older man, not responding to this last provocation, crossed his arms one over the other.

"I propose, General, that we each pick a champion from among our respective members, first."

"No general am I, but a master sergeant seeing fifteen years of command and war in the King's service."

"Okay, Major," came the irreverent retort, "pick a champion amongst you, first, before we spell out the terms of contest, as we select our own."

Both groups went into quiet and respective conference.

The veterans' group picked their strongest and ablest fighter as their champion. They selected the giant standing with them who, by his very size, emanated his own special aura of power.

With a nod to the young spokesman, the other eight recruits indicated their own choice after a brief discussion with one another about whom they were going to pick for the position. They chose Pall.

Two spokesmen and two champions moved closer to each other with the table still between them.

"Your challenge and terms are..." indicated the veteran.

"They are a challenge using the mind as the arms of our wits, and riddles will be posed to each champion as combat weapons would be used in close fighting on the field. The one besting the other by his inability to correctly answer the posed statement loses by default. Ergo, becoming loser and server to the others as previously stated in this parley: Agreed?"

Laughter widely broke out throughout the tavern as customers, workers and the tavern keeper himself realized that the nature of combat was by engagement of mind rather than one of brute force.

The elder spokesman and his group's champion turned red in their faces. "Agreed," said the leader, and then added with contempt, "Your youth has left you callow and callous in manner."

The leader of the recruits glibly retorted, "Your age has left your phallus fallow and without stamina."

At this juncture in the battle of insults, every recruit and veteran started to prepare for a physical brawl. They aggressively began seeking the fastest way to do so.

The young spokesman jumped on top of the table, interrupting the momentum of all to start a fight. He grandly waved the champions of both sides to sit opposite one another at the table.

Looking out at the crowd now gathering round to witness more directly the contest, he asked them, "Who has a coin they wish to use to see who goes first with the question to be posed to the other?"

Men reached quickly into their pockets, but were too late in getting them as a gold coin was sent sailing over to the recruit standing on the table. One of the young serving women had also jumped on another table. She adroitly sent her previous night's payment for pleasure rendered soaring over the heads of many to the young man. He deftly caught the coin and sent it back to her.

"Thank you, fair maiden," he said sincerely to her, "but pray thee, keep yon coin and flip it for us to see who goes forth first in this campaign."

Applause burst forth from every pair of hands in the room at this gracious gesture in praising womanhood and beauty. Yet, comment and reciprocating acclaim for it further maddened each of the eleven veterans in contest against the nine recruits.

"Age like yours seldom has advantages, but in this all–to–be–brief exchange, we let you call the fall of the coin's outcome," the spokesman said to the elder champion.

The young man snapped his middle finger and thumb together on his left hand so loudly that the serving girl simultaneously flipped the coin high in the air over her head. "The King's hallowed crown," said the champion of the veterans in a deep bass voice, as the coin reached the highest point of its arc in midair.

It landed in her outstretched hand. She showed the result of the toss to others to confirm her call, singing forth, "Castle, not crown, landed in my hand."

The crowd, now at a fever pitch to see this duel play itself out before them, blatantly and uproariously called forth its betting on the results. Odds now favored the recruits because Pall would be the one to ask the first conundrum.

Instead, after the betting quieted down, Pall flatly stated, "I defer the winning of the toss to my opponent."

The room went silent. Approval of his generosity broke out in scattered response throughout the tavern. Realizing what he had done in giving the giant opposite him the chance to offer the first question, laughter and general applause enthusiastically erupted from everyone there— except from Pall's opponents.

The wagering over both groups battling over the right to the table in front of them reached a fever pitch.

Pall waited patiently for it to become quieter. When the room almost fell silent, he looked over to the warrior seated across from him and simply said to him, "Proceed."

The veteran, looking uncomfortable, started out in an unsure voice, which grew stronger at last toward the end of his question. "I have skin: more eyes than one. I can be very good when I am done. What am I?"

Without hesitation, Pall answered, "A potato."

The older man frowned and hit his right fist powerfully down on top of the table in frustration. The table shuddered. Wood split where his closed hand slammed down onto it.

The crowd roared with hand–clapping catcalls and the exchanging of money on who had won the first riddle.

To match the jejune level of his opponent's question, Pall stated, "Weight in my belly, trees on my back, nails in my ribs, feet do I lack."

The veteran screwed up his eyes in his head, bit his lips and concentrated on finding the answer to Pall's riddle. The warrior opened his eyes and looked at one of his companions to his left.

The companion silently mouthed one word.

The older champion smiled without humor and uttered, "Ship."

Boos broke out, but Pall said, "Answer granted."

The younger spokesman crowed to the crowd exclaiming to all, "And now who is foul and fowled!"

Again, men began to lunge at one another.

Pall stood up and the giant facing him did likewise. Silence reigned in the room.

"Your turn to ask me," Pall stated softly.

"What goes up and down the tavern stairs without moving," the man quickly asked.

"The wood that went into making them," instantly came Pall's response.

The big man gritted his teeth in impatient anger, flexed his shoulders and biceps in frustration. He nodded, "Yes," to Pall.

Again, betting and the exchange of money reached another high point.

Quiet restored itself inside the tavern.

The young champion queried his opponent, "My life can be measured in a quarter of the night. I serve by being devoured. If thin, I am quick." He paused. Looking at his opponent, he indicated with a nod of his head at him saying, "If fat, I am slow. Wind is my foe. What am I?"

The giant, burning now with Pall's insult and disrespect being thrown at him, stood up. He leaned over to the other ten veterans.

One gave him an answer.

Smirking and stretching the full length of his frame, he said, "Candle."

"Another fowl, you cow!" shouted Pall's spokesman at the giant standing before him. No outside consultation is allowed."

The giant shrugged his shoulders and said, "Take a swing at me and I'll show you a riddle you won't even wake up to."

The young spokesman went for a sword that was not at his hip.

The giant laughed.

Four men, two from either side jumped onto the table itself.

Pall stood up and waved them down. "Accepted," he said.

No one said a word in the tavern. No money exchanged hands.

The four men reluctantly came down off the table and returned to their original places.

Pall sat back down on the bench before the table. With a small gesture of his left hand, he said, "Your turn."

The veterans' champion screwed up his face, concentrating mightily. He smiled having selected the riddle he thought was an excellent one. "You use a knife to chop off my head and weep beside me once I am dead," he said, emphasizing the last word in particular.

"Onion," Pall answered before his opponent took another breath. "Pray, sit down. Relax."

The giant sat down slowly. "Ask your childish riddle, but it's your last," he rumbled.

The young man looked at him intently, posing the following question, "What must you always buy, but never want to use?"

The older warrior became uncomfortable. He looked at his companions, but they could not provide their champion this time with an answer.

Everyone else in the room remained completely quiet. All betting ceased. Indeed, it was forgotten over the intensity of the moment.

"I don't know," eventually said the veteran.

Pall smiled ruefully and said, "Coffin."

The giant stood up slightly. "Yes, smart jackass that you are; and, that's what I will gladly put you in." He reached over swiftly for a man his size. Picking Pall up in two hands, he hauled him over the table and enfolded Pall into a chest squeeze in his massive arms.

The older soldier laughed and made sounds as if he were eating a meal. The other veterans laughed along with their champion.

The recruits were stunned at this sudden reversal of fortune. They did nothing but watch in alarm to what was happening in front of them.

Pall's right arm for some reason got free of the giant hug of death enfolding him. Before anyone could see what happened, the young man had snapped his clenched fist into the warrior's neck just to the right side and below his voice box.

The goliath laughed off the strike and squeezed harder.

People could see the young man give a half smile within what appeared to be an embrace of death.

Holding Pall against him, the giant moved away from the table as if he had a place to put the young recruit. However, the older champion stopped in

134

completing such a movement. He looked confused. His tight death grip on Pall relaxed, allowing Pall to pull the veteran's arms away.

Stepping out of the circle of the giant's arms, Pall stood back from him, roughly appraising him with a questioning look.

The warrior tried to cough. He gurgled some sort of statement. He turned completely red in the face, and would have fallen onto the table if it had not been for five of his companions preventing him from collapsing there.

Blood started pouring out of his mouth in time with the rhythm of his heartbeat. His attempts at speaking all failed him in a chorus of gurgling and burbling sounds. The rapid movement of the warrior's eyes revealed, initially, curiosity and wonder over what had just happened to him. Soon, his eyes held a startled look. He could not breathe. His gaze, in turn, changed from blank, to dul... to empty. His spirit turned inward. His eyes remained open. The warrior's body convulsed twice, and then went rigid.

The giant's brothers-in-arms silently placed his great form onto the table before him.

There was a stunned silence.

No one in the room, except for a single individual, had ever seen such a sight like this one happen before them.

From deep within the crowd, a voice sounded in wonder, "One punch: He killed the giant with one blow of his fist!"

Other individuals around the tavern took up the cry. Many people started, or attempted, to push their way into the area where the contest was just held in order to take a closer look at the dead veteran lying on the table, the combatants themselves and Pall. Complete pandemonium began erupting throughout the crowd.

Pall's fellow recruits quietly gathered at the four cardinal points around him.

With a mutual shout of outrage, the ten remaining veterans made to turn on their younger foes to engage them in a physical fight to the death.

Before they could do so, and before the customers throughout the tavern could react in a complete and utter uproar, the crack of a ceremonial baton could be clearly heard resonating around the room from its being expertly struck onto the top of another table nearby the combatants.

A lithe looking, middle–aged man stood up on the table where he had been seated. He was dressed in the uniform of a high ranking officer. His demeanor brooked no dissent from anyone in the room.

Everything and everyone, once again, became completely stilled.

People near enough to the dead champion could hear the blood draining out of the giant's mouth and dripping onto the floor.

Pall, seeing the senior officer for the first time, was struck immediately with the thought, *He acts like my father.*

"Most of you in this room know me," declared the officer.

"For those who don't, I am High Marshall Solace Umbré. I command an elite unit of men called the Aeonians."

Turning to the fully armed men at his table, he said to them, "Clear the room: all but for the youngster there who threw such a doughty and fortune–esteemed blow. Bring him over to me for questioning when you're done."

CHAPTER THIRTEEN

Fifteen Aeonians hurried to the task given them. They had no difficulties following their commander's orders as most everyone became docile before them. The tavern keeper, his family and his workers were sent temporarily to the rooms upstairs. The customers were led to the door and were perfunctorily ushered away. They were told in definitive terms to leave the premises and not return back to the area for at least a day.

Ten veterans remained.

Pall and his eight companions stayed in place throughout the whole time the tavern was being cleared.

A dozen Aeonians ringed both groups while the other three guarded the doors into the tavern. Another twelve entered the tavern from where they had been stationed outside and took their respective places beside their peers.

With baton in hand, Umbré climbed down the tabletop from where he had commanded the crowd. He approached the veteran soldiers' spokesman. Standing before him and looking him straight in the eyes, he evenly said, "Master Sergeant, my thanks to you for remaining in the room with us. I want you to stay within two throws of a war hammer from my command tent. If I have any further need of you, you will be summoned to me there. You and your men are dismissed."

Saluting the High Marshall sharply, the master sergeant called for a general salute from the rest of his men, which they sharply snapped off to Umbré. They left the building with surprising speed, especially for men who desired that revenge be sorely meted out against the nine recruits for their part in the death of their champion.

Umbré sat back down on the bench from which he had arisen to address the departed veteran master sergeant.

The ring of elite soldiers around the recruits tightened more.

It became completely silent throughout the room.

Guards shifted on their feet, displacing their weight for comfort and efficiency both, in case action was to be called upon them by their commander.

For a span of two dozen beats of the heart, the Marshall looked down at his hands. He looked at the nails of both his hands in a sort of bemused, abstracted way.

"You know," he deliberated to the recruits aloud, and with his gaze on Pall, "What you did to him," indicating the dead man on the table, "is something I witnessed done about twenty–two years ago."

139

No one in the room replied to this statement.

"It was done by a man for whom you look a spitting image when he was your age."

Pall returned a worried glance at his companions, and a puzzled look at the man seated before him.

The High Marshall dropped his left hand to his side with the right one remaining palm down on the table. "Captain," he addressed the man nearest him in the circle around the recruits, "at ease. Escort these eight recruits surrounding their young rooster here to yon table. Summon the owner of this fine establishment and have him see that they are given some of the tavern's finest ale. Place the cost of the same on my bill for this evening."

Pall nodded almost imperceptibly to his companions that it was okay for them to relax. He remained standing in place.

The Marshall's orders were carried out immediately by his soldiers without any ill will occurring to despoil the efficiency in which they were executed.

After the recruits were settled and served, the Marshall had his men stand down. He bade his captain and another eight men remain in the room, but at ease. The rest were sent out into the street to help cordon off the area.

"Pray you," he said to Pall directly, "you may approach and be seated to my right."

The young man raised his eyes in slight surprise.

Umbré saw the young man's hesitation and waved him over next to him with some irritation openly conveyed on the Marshall's expression.

For some reason, Pall felt no fear that a reprisal would occur. He deferentially approached the officer and waited again for the Marshall to indicate Pall should be seated next to Umbré's right side.

After he gestured the young man be seated next to him, the Marshall called for the tavern keeper. He ordered two flagons of ale be brought over to them. Upon drinks being served, the Marshall took his and quenched his thirst deeply from the flagon before him. He bade Pall do likewise to the drink before him as well, to which the young man complied eagerly.

Umbré smacked his lips together to indicate his satisfaction with his drink. He politely belched. Looking at the baton resting on the table before him, he said, more than asked, Pall, "You're the son of High Commander David Warren."

Looking surprised and curious at his statement, Pall simply complied with it by saying, "Yes, Sir."

The Marshall slightly nodded to Pall's response to him. Taking another drink from his ale that had just been refilled by the tavern keeper, Umbré mused aloud, "Last time I saw him you were three years of age."

Pall knotted his brows. He could not recall ever seeing this man or hearing his name mentioned in the Warren home. For that matter, he never knew his father held such an exalted position in the King's army.

The Marshall watched the young man before him trying to sort out what was just so flatly stated to him. "Your first name is Pall, with a double L; and I believe, when you became older, you apprenticed with him," he announced, "to serve before the forge and to serve in armed practice."

Pall unconsciously stood up to attention.

Umbré's captain bestirred himself from near the front entrance to the tavern and started walking over to the table where his commander remained seated.

The Marshall respectfully waved his captain away and said to Pall, "You are free to respond to what I just said."

"I did not know my father held the position of High Commander of the King's Northern Armies. He never made reference to the level of command he reached in the army. How do you know him?" Pall asked.

Umbré picked up the baton. He studied it carefully. "Your father and I," he said after a significant pause, "were recruits together. We became the closest of friends, then bitter rivals over a stunningly beautiful woman."

"This woman was my mother?" Pall softly inquired.

The Marshall nodded. "Here, sit down, young Warren," he commanded gently.

Pall complied with the order.

Umbré could see that Pall wanted more information. "Your mother was the most unique woman I have ever met, or even seen, for that matter," he obligingly said. "She's... was... from the Western Isles and part of another visiting king's family at the time we first saw her. A first daughter, in fact, of that king...." The Marshall stopped talking. His eyes had a faraway look to them.

Catching himself dwelling in memories past, especially in uniform, he shook his head quickly side to side several times. "Long time ago," he said to no one in particular.

He refocused his eyes to the present and checked the room scanning the whole area. His attention alighted on Pall's companions. "These recruits need to be lightly escorted back to their training camp, Captain," he said. "See to it," he added.

The Captain quickly called over two of his men, who then likewise escorted the recruits out the door and into the street back toward their bivouacs.

Marshall Umbré ordered two meals be brought to his table from the owner. He also told his captain to retrieve the rest of the man's family, servants and workers back to their respective jobs and places in the tavern.

The older man picked up the baton and held it before him in his sword hand. "He, your father, High Commander of the King's Northern Armies, gave me this." Umbré chuckled and said, "We not only were fierce competitors vying for the attention of your mother, but also continued to be the same in training, being promoted through the ranks, on the battlefield and even on leave away from the military interests of the realm.

Solace paused a moment, lost in thought, memories and the flush of what youth gave him in his past. "We became bitter enemies with one another," he added with a sigh of regret.

The Marshall looked inquiringly at the young recruit at his side, particularly to see if Pall had any questions or something the young man wanted to say to the older one.

The young man remained respectfully quiet.

"This baton," he said in a slight suggestion of awe, "had remained in the King's treasury for almost two hundred years. No man, neither officer or soldier, nor civilian, was believed by the royal powers during that time to be worthy and deserving in having it given into such a would–be champion's, or potential victor's, hand."

The tavern keeper and his wife came over to the Marshall's table bearing the food the senior officer had ordered.

The Captain also approached the table. "Would you like me to serve you, Marshall?" he asked his commander.

"It's all right, Martains," Umbré answered. "Pray see to the men, and yourself, for something to eat and a drink or two to refresh your strength for this evening's business. Leave guards at the doors on the first floor. Maintain perimeter security as well and see that we are not disturbed."

"Yes, Sir!" the Captain replied. He snapped to attention and saluted his commander. Martains carried out his orders and gathered his men together in another room to give the Marshall privacy.

The two men, alone in the large room in the tavern, silently ate their food.

Again, the tavern keeper and his demure wife came to the table, cleared it and refilled both men's tankards. "Is there anything else that your Honor requires?" he asked Umbré.

The Marshall shook his head, saying, "No, my friend, you have outdone yourself this night. The food was hearty and filling. The drink provides the goodness of Morpheus and the seductive bite of Calypso on reviving the spirits of a man. Serve us another round of ale and then pray retire for the evening."

The tavern keeper and his wife bowed to the Marshall. The wife said, "We most humbly thank you and remain in your debt, your Honor, especially in saving our home and business from being ruined earlier this day."

"You are most welcome," said Umbré. "I am afraid I did so for the most selfish of reasons. Had I refrained from interfering in this young man's contest of half riddles and half–wits, I might next not have had a place such as this one to come to at the end of a long day, or at the beginning of an even longer night."

Once more, the man and his wife bowed, but even deeper than before, to the officer. Without saying anything more, they quickly left the room.

The Marshall took a drink of his ale, urging Pall to do the same. Looking at Pall, he smiled softly. "We seem to have a mutual problem here, young man," he said.

"Yes, Sir," Pall agreed.

"I have to mete out discipline for what occurred in this room, and you and your fellow recruits have to be the recipients of said punishment."

"Yes, Sir," Pall again agreed.

"Glad to see you are in accord with my last statement, lad. What do you think is a just sentence for you and yours?"

"Marshall, I trust your decision will be appropriately adjudicated."

The older man laughed, saying, "Said just as your father would have declaimed."

Pall took a drink along with the Marshall.

The older man turned serious, officially saying, "Yon member of my elite unit in his final rest on that table was one of the best of my shock troops. He will not easily be replaced. The coup d'état you delivered so severely to him was a feat of wonder to most, but a gesture of unfortunate waste. I leave it to you to decide the outcome of this predicament; I will speak for the veterans' champion and for this man whom you bested out of regretful self–defense.

"The final question posed to you, the final riddle of this day you must answer, is this: now that this conundrum has been created, what must be done to solve it with honor and righteousness?"

Without any hesitation, Pall stated, "As I am the one whose hand struck this man, I request that my fellow companions and I serve you for the remainder of your term as the King's High Marshall. I request that I, or those in my company, fill the place of the giant that is slain before us."

"Fairly presented," Umbré blandly said. "No matter how well and suitable your nascent proclamation may seem so apt to you, you and yours are but mere recruits, nevertheless, and still groveling for mastery of the basics of what it means to be a soldier. Now, you make claim to enter a select group of men and warriors exclusive of the fact you are mere children claiming to be ready to fill the shoes of weapons masters and combat veterans. What say you to this characterization?"

"I, and my fellow recruits, are in our final week of training. As we are but youngsters practicing in the company of seasoned soldiers and hardened veterans, I petition you, Sir, to allow us to complete our initial training. Once done successfully, take us into your ranks on a trial basis of another training phase equal to the one we are finishing. When this has been accomplished, send me four of your best men to test me, and an equivalent number, likewise, to my other eight companions."

"So be it said," the High Marshall intoned.

"So be it finished," the emerging soldier before him concluded.

CHAPTER FOURTEEN

Clouds obscured the sun. Lost in the memory that had taken him back in time, he had not seen the shift in the sky going from a dazzling, deep blue in color to one in which major cumulus clouds had completely blocked out the sun. Cast in a grayer, daytime light, the Sentinel Trees around him shared their own brilliance with one another, such that they emanated a glow of crimson and purple that soothed his troubled spirit. Their trunks shone as well, but in muted silver tones. The wind, while not steady, was fitful. An occasionally strong gust would encounter the trees by flinging their leaves upward because of its shearing away from the ground back toward the sky above them.

Pall now felt like a ghost. *I am like a man whose spirit is split in two, traveling unknowingly in this world while treading the incomplete paths of forgotten memories.*

Recalling the memory of the giant he had slain when but a mere recruit in the King's army, he also realized, with a shock of recognition, how similar in stature Savage was to this giant.

No wonder, when I first espied John Savage, I first saw him with a dim awareness of his likeness in another.

Pall worried that perhaps he had killed Savage's brother, or another member of his family. *I yet see darkly into who I really am. Let alone find a thread of logic through this knot of despair....* These thoughts put him into further despondency.

He physically shook the melancholy spirit away from him. Pall forced himself to pay attention to where he was in the woods. He looked around him and was again struck by the beauty and grandeur of the copper beeches that stood nearby. He recalled the position of the sun in the sky. Seeing the point above him where he guessed the sun was now, he saw no need to keep going through an untracked wood. Pall decided that he could retrace his steps back to the path onto which he had raced on foot off of the wagon road when Merek and he had run away from Ünger in opposite directions from one another.

The young man also realized his throat was parched. He could not recollect when he had last had a drink of water. While he had a limited amount of food, he still needed water to help keep him alive.

If I can get onto the path and then find the wagon road, I should be able to find a stream, he said to himself. *If I am fortunate, I might also find Merek.*

Without too much difficulty, and only being turned around once, he soon discovered the path. He even found several of his footprints from the night before still pressed down into the verdant grass on the edge of the path in a couple of places. The cumulus formation of clouds above started to lessen in number. They were being overwhelmed by the appearance of long, fragmented streams of cirrus clouds. Eventually, a combination of the two types of clouds occurred. Wispy streams of white joined with a thin, sheet like set of clouds.

Pall smiled ironically because the sun shone dully through this diaphanous ribbon in the sky.

Like a pall had been thrown underneath the light of the sun's rays, he admitted to himself.

Soon, he heard the trickle of water nearby. Locating the source of the sound, he discovered a small spring bubbling out of a bed of rocks. The sound he had heard was made by water falling into a small pool not even two feet around in circumference. He fell onto his stomach and drank the achingly pure and refreshing liquid until his thirst was satisfied. Pall decided that this was a good spot in which to rest, as well as a chance to eat a bit more food and drink some more water. He wished he had a waterproof skin in which he could carry some for later use when he needed it.

Before lying down on his left side, he drew his sword and placed it within easy reach of his right hand, being sure that his scabbard was out of the way. He brought the pack next to him and sampled some of the remaining dried fruit and meat. He turned over onto his back and looked up at the trees and sky above him. Despite telling himself that he needed to be very cautious about his surroundings, he fell asleep. Whether or not he tumbled back into his memories or plunged into a remembered dream, he was unable to determine the difference. Pall welcomed the relief of being away from where he was when awake.

They had been in their—now—second phase of training in the Aeonian camp for almost two weeks. Marshall Umbré had assigned them under the care of Captain Joseph Martains. The Captain, in turn, placed them in the hands of his best two sergeants; Sergeant Meginhard, was the one who trained them during the day, and Sergeant Burchard, was the other who tested them at night.

The Captain agreed with the two sergeants and the Marshall as well, that these nine men were being watched and judged by everyone in the elite force in which they were newly, and perhaps, temporarily "visiting" at the time.

Physical conditioning was a steady, and ever increasing, daily event. They were made to do stand–alone training for several hours at a time with a variety of weapons, such as daggers and knives, various types of swords, blunt weapons and spears and other polearms and axes.

Hand–to–hand combat experience was not permitted them, yet.

They were given, instead, forced marches, running, drilling, more forced marches and other extreme forms of physical exercise, along with heavy doses of verbal grief from their trainers. Evaluations of their prowess and progress were made by the two sergeants. These were sent to Captain Martains, along with other anecdotal information from other men in the surrounding Aeonian unit who had contact with the recruits.

Grief from "their" sergeants was a given expectation. This training, too, increased in its applied rigor toward the young men. The basic training they had just recently passed to get into the King's army now seemed like a children's game to them. Meginhard and Burchard went out of their way to harass them at all hours of the day and night. The two sergeants were using a typical, double team strategy of harassment on the recruits. Meginhard was merciless, brusque and sarcastic; Burchard was less merciless, less brusque and very sarcastic.

Pall and his eight companions were sick of hearing from their instructors, "Screw courage, daring, or anything special; it's about attitude, persistence and discipline!"

The young men knew, though, that all this treatment was meted out liberally to see if any of

153

them could rise to a level of mental toughness and endurance wherein they were in control of their emotions. Exemplary and prompt behavior on their part was critical to the success of sound decision making and teamwork, particularly in men who were also in superb physical condition.

As part of their solidarity in being one functioning unit, they daily held strategy discussions with one another. The purpose of these brief conversations was to help ensure their victory in entering this elite army unit. Topics ranged from taking care of their feet to improving their mastery at weapons handling.

Sergeant Burchard had told them one evening that he and Meginhard were designing their final tests. They would be given at the end of their training. The recruits knew that combined physical and mental tests would be given them. These tests were going to be arduous, demanding and brutal. They also knew that the sergeants were in the process of respectively assigning the best Aeonian fighters to oppose them. Burchard and Meginhard were seeking those veterans who not only were the best fighters, but those wanting to eke complete woe and revenge upon Pall and his companions for the death of their fellow companion Savaric by, literally, Pall's hand.

To a man, every veteran soldier in this unit wanted to be one of the thirty–six men chosen. All of these warriors saw this whole affair as something that was beyond the audacity of regular, unqualified recruits showboating themselves into the elite Aeonian ranks. For these grizzled combat soldiers, this was a war that had to be won unconditionally. The fact that it was begun against them by the audacity of green recruits in a tavern smarted enough; for it to have been negotiated one–on–one between the High Marshall and Pall was beyond reason. It violated their trust in the command structure and ran against the grain of cohesiveness in their brotherhood.

Pall had not seen the High Marshall since the contest in the tavern. Martains, he saw from a distance twice. However, one early morning, the Captain had approached Sergeant Meginhard while the nine men were in position at the beginning of a forced, fifteen–mile march in full armor and equipment.

The meeting took place at the open end of their cantonment.

None other than Meginhard heard the message delivered him personally by the senior commander. With his message delivered, Umbré quickly left the field with his guard closely following in back of him. Martains was nowhere to be seen on this occasion.

Sergeant Meginhard sent for a runner who, after hearing the sergeant's orders, promptly ran off the field to parts known only to the Marshall, the sergeant and now the messenger. Meginhard, with extra power in his lungs, shouted at the recruits— and their accompanying two dozen guards—to begin their march at double speed.

Two miles later into the march, the sergeant eased their pace to a steady walk. Despite the early morning chill, the men were sweating profusely. No talking was allowed.

The recruits, however, did not let this order of silence gag them into muteness alone. They continued communicating with one another by hand signals that they devised in the last week of basic training. This idea to do so came from Jarin, the spokesman of the recruits. "After all," he had said to them at that time, "the Aeonian contingent will do everything in its power to divide, silence and defeat us. They'll exhaust us physically and mentally. I'll teach you the silent language of the woman servant who raised my sister and me. She talked with her hands. In less than three days, you'll learn basic signs and their meaning so we can talk with one another."

By the second week of *talking* in this fashion, which was the first week of being in the Aeonian camp, all eight recruits could *speak* as well as Jarin.

Since the start of this march, they had been communicating in such a manner. They offered encouragement and advice to one another, while also heaping much scornful ridicule onto the sergeant.

Meginhard, not fully aware that this form of communication was being used among the recruits, still felt its presence tangentially. He could not understand why this group of young men was withstanding the mental and physical pressures being employed against them so well. His training instincts were alert and fine tuned to the wiliness and slyness of trainees.

Even though these lads are not talking, I can feel their laughter on my account, he thought in frustration to himself.

This feeling of nonverbal sabotage being levied by them against the sergeant only increased in its intensity as the morning wore on. Soon the pace was ratcheted up to a quick–time step and held at that level for an additional three miles.

At the end of the fifth mile, Meginhard began a non–stop barrage of ridicule and verbal abuse against them.

It had no deleterious effect on the young men. If anything, they increased their pace instead, which now began not only to make the sergeant furious, but befuddled him as well.

Two more miles were gained. The sergeant had alerted all the guards to keep their attention on the nine recruits to see if anything untoward was being committed by them. Nothing out of the ordinary could be ascertained. Ridicule turned into rancor. Epithets turned into threats.

Suddenly, the extraordinary broke out. The recruits started chanting while they strode together in time down the dirt track upon which they were marching:

"Left, right, left more:
the sergeant we adore;
shouts left, yells right:
gets us ready for war.

Guard left, watch right:
he's all that and more;
we run, we fight:
who do we do it for?

Shake it a left, that's right:
Meginhard's his name;
he's tough, he's rough:
he's beggin' hard for fame:

Left, right, left more:
the sergeant we adore.
Shouts left, yells right:
gets us ready for war."

There was not one guard without a smile on his face. These veterans could not help themselves as they broke out into suppressed laughter and restrained guffaws.

The sergeant lost what composure he had left in him. He immediately called a halt and ordered a circle be put around the nine "singing fools." He stood them in a line.

Making sure he had everyone's undivided attention, he bellowed, "I know you boys think I'm working on half–rations up here," he pointed to his head. "You may think you know everything. You may think you have me over an empty barrel of ale. I know what you think of me, my orders and my name, especially."

The sergeant ran up in front of Pall. Turning beet red in the face, he snarled, "You especially, 'One–Blow Pall'. Maybe you'd like to take care of my Meginhard. Let's see you stroke me like you did Savaric! But that's not goin to happen. I'll take you in the throat and turn you into a wench for sure."

Pall made himself focus in the distance just to the left of the sergeant's right ear. He remained as motionless as he could during this tirade.

"And that goes for the rest of you, too. I'm not called Meginhard for nothin," he blustered. "I'll make it real hard on you, but not the way you young bucks think.

"I want two guards on either side of each of these nine trouvères, with two in back and two at the head of the column," he said mockingly to them.

When Jarin raised his eyes at the word *trouvères*, the sergeant chanted, "trou–ba–dours, to you fish; that's left, that's right...."

Twenty–two Aeonian warriors sprang into the places they were ordered, while all nine recruits picked up the pace again in time with the sergeant's cadence.

"As a matter of fact," he continued, as he jogged alongside them, "conditions change in war and on the field of battle as it does here on my say–so: Accordingly, the distance you march now is doubled."

Meginhard was smiling wickedly when he said, "I want the other two guards around this one," he indicated with a nod of his head at Pall. "If he even stumbles, you four knock him on his arse."

With everyone in motion, Meginhard sarcastically said to them, "Ain't that pretty: eight masters of nothin and their blowhard boy wonder all marchin to my tune!"

Looking aside at some of the dour expressions on his guards' faces, the sergeant attempted to soothe his men while continuing to rankle the young recruits, saying, "Get it straight, some high rankin and coin–heavy fools might call us with the soubriquet of the Aeonians, but that's a pussy name," he gloated. "Among us, and to our enemies, we're called the Onions because our enemies weep while we wage war against them. I'm here now to make sure if your eyes don't spill water, your feet damn will."

———————+—•

A twig snapped in two, not less than twenty feet away from where he had fallen asleep.

Pall scrambled onto his feet and stood next to the bole of a massive copper beech. He listened carefully for other telltale signs that someone, or something, was nearby him. Soon enough, he saw motion to the left side of him in the woods, which came to a stop not less than ten feet away. Remaining on the other side of the tree away from the man who now appeared in the small glade where he had been resting, Pall saw someone who, at this close distance away, smelled like offal; or worse yet, a man who smelled like human excrement. He moved in a way that made Pall liken him to someone else he had just recently met. Nonetheless, this individual moved in fright and not in confidence. He kept looking back over his shoulder from where he had walked.

161

A man in green, he thought. *But this man is in brown.* Pall almost burst out in laughter. This was Error before him. The young man remembered that Carac had told them he had seen Error hide himself in a privy back at the farmstead.

The levity Pall was feeling upon sight of the besmirched man immediately lessened. *If Error is scared of something following him,* he considered silently, *that means it has to be Ünger who is hunting him.*

He let Error move by him unseen. At first sight of him, Pall felt pity for the man, despite what was done to Pall at the behest of the now brown man. He would have tried to befriend Error. Be that as it may, any chance that the demon beast was in close proximity coursing after the Captain, made thoughts of good will towards him disappear.

Pall tried to think what kind of creature Ünger was like. He had never seen, or at least could recall at the present time, anything like it.

First, it's there, then it's not there. It's visible, then invisible. It's formless, then has form. It swirls into place, then disappears before your eyes.

Pall smiled again, despite the seriousness of the situation. He thought, *Sounds like a riddle. If I had known of such a creature when I was a recruit, I would have used it on Savaric.*

The young man continued to puzzle his mind over the beast. *Where does such a thing come from?*

If I ever meet Herald again, I must question him about it.

As he was thinking about these extraordinary things, he wondered what the Valravn's statement meant when it flew at him when he was with Savage seeing the farmstead for his first time.

He wondered, *Is it a foretelling? Are the events recited by the bird going to happen to me?*

He repeated the raven's prediction in his mind.

Shaking his head with uncertainty, he again started to replay the telling of the prophecy, as well as wanting to reconsider what Savage had said to him about the Valravn.

Error had disappeared from view, leaving a faint foulness behind in his passing.

A cricket sounded in the area where Error had first appeared. Pall felt as though he had stepped into a cobweb. Yet, he had been standing still; no possible contact on his part was made with such a gossamer object. He heard the high pitched droning of a mosquito inside his head....

Pall brought to mind Savage's advice when encountering Ünger.

Staying on the same side of the copper beech as he had been when Error almost encountered him, Pall closed his eyes and let his mind go blank.

CHAPTER FIFTEEN

John Savage, for all of his almost seven feet of height, ran swiftly from the wattle fenced in herb garden where he had just left Pall in Twin's care. He wanted to reach the closest part of the great forest that was around the farm. He was eagerly anticipating returning to the Demesne of the Sentinels. Savage loved being around the copper beeches. It was only in the Wood of the Royal Guard that he attained a peace and sense of comfort he found nowhere else. He knew that once he entered it his sense of balance and the right order of things soon would be restored.

Certainly I will think better there than the hell around me now.

Of all the concerns facing him at this moment, his worry for Pall's wellbeing still tugged at him. He hoped that Pall and Twin were able to get away safely from the farmstead.

His attention, however, had to turn to his present circumstances and predicament. The moon's light was more than sufficient for him to cross the farmstead proper and attain the edge of the forest. As he ran towards the woodland, he could see his shadow outlined sharply in front of him.

Screams, begging and gurgling sounds from those being taken down by Ünger and his divisions reached him as he was heading through the field. Hollow echoes of this struggle reverberated off buildings behind him and bounced off the wall of woods he was approaching. Savage felt fortunate he was not one of those men in the clutches of Ünger's horror.

Nothing, at least no inimical force or creature, followed him.

Perhaps, he thought, *the lad's song has given me some protection and I am able to get into these sacred woods.*

Reaching the divide between farm and wood, Savage plunged deeper into the forest. His goal was to get as far into its depths as he could go before sunrise. Perhaps he could even catch a moment or two of rest, as well as catch something to eat later on when it was first light. The bowman, like Pall, had not eaten anything for at least twenty–four hours.

In his flight toward safer ground, Savage could not but help, once again, to admire the wood through which he was moving. Even in the light of the moon, maybe even more so than in the daytime, the rugged looking trees seem to emanate a radiance of strength, peace and protective assurance that all would be well.

He felt them watching him from a distant place. *After all*, he mused to himself pensively, *some of you hale old Sentinels are at least two or three hundred years of age.*

Before he was aware of what he was doing, he had stopped before a very old tree. He was dimly aware that he had unslung his bow and quiver. The bowman also unstrapped his sword and scabbard, placing them next to his longbow as well. He placed these weapons against the base of the tree and sat down on the ground with his back against the old copper beech. He was between a series of large roots emerging from the tree for a distance of about four or five feet before dipping back into the well-drained soil again.

A surprising thought came to him—fluttered truly by him—*like a butterfly*, the big man smiled. He realized with a start that he was like a child against the side of a giant presence. He felt small but ensconced within a fortress of ancient power.

The archer's eyes closed, fluttered open briefly. Closed again.

In the pre–light just before dawn, the first Ünger found Savage deeply asleep in the copper tree's embrace. It approached him stealthily. Neither sound nor movement could be heard by the human ear. The creature had been looking steadily for the rest of the mortals who had escaped its predation on them. After taking its time and full delight in consuming all of the men it annihilated, it maintained mental contact with the presence of its two other divisions. The beast sent them on a variety of mop–up chores to certify that every human present at the farmstead was accounted for and consumed.

To Ünger, its sense of destruction served as a grand ministry. To massacre life was equal to a high mass where death became a wondrous experience. Committing itself to such a calling was a telic force that could not be denied in and of itself. Ünger was made for such a purpose. Consumption of the force emanating from humans provided it with pure energy to help fuel its hatred of anything living.

Savage was a mystery to it.

An internal vibration of a sort went through Ünger. It wasn't truly a thought. It was more like an intimation: *This breather protects the singer.*

The nefarious creature discerned a different kind of power in the man that he had yet encountered in one of his kind. Its gourmet sense of human delectability was aroused. It first wanted to assay this man form called Savage more consummately before destroying it. As Ünger came into the circle of the copper beech's root system, two things happened to it simultaneously. It sensed the presence of not only another entity, but one of vast power and vigor. It also began to smell something burning.

Never experiencing doubt or fear before, the malicious beast became angry and curious at the same time over these two new impressions. It felt thwarted in its purpose, but it could not tell why it felt this way. It continued its cautious approach toward Savage. However, each movement toward the big man sapped Ünger's energy. Surprisingly, and by the time it stood completely over the human, it felt spent, enervated by what it was trying to do.

The beast attempted to start its killing mechanism. Nothing in itself could trigger the process to begin. It tried to make a sound. Any sound. It failed utterly for the first time in its memory to do even that simple gesture. It tried once more to howl. Instead, a whimper feebly burped out its mouth. For some reason the monster could not fathom, this last measure of strength being denied it, infuriated it even more. Nevertheless, its fury was futile and less than tepid in its ability to force any harm against the bowman. It actually started to feel cold deep in the pit of its gut.

Ünger attempted to communicate with the other two divisions of itself. It failed miserably.

With growing amazement, and with increasing consternation, the creature felt deprived of its source of energy. It became filled with torpor. Its mind became dull and ground to a halt. Stooped over Savage's sleeping body, Ünger slept as well, but its sleep was the slumber of ultimate silence.

———❖——

The bowman opened his eyes. The sounds of birds singing, insects droning around him and the wind moving through the leaves in the tree above him filled him with a sense of peace. It was full daylight. He looked up into the canopy of the tree he was under and froze into place. The monster from the farm was above him. By the look of it, Ünger was about to play its mischief on him.

Savage felt like a fool for being caught out in the open so easily. He felt as if he had betrayed himself and the trust into which he had been placed by the King.

The archer held his breath for the initial strike to begin. But nothing happened. The creature above him was frozen in place with either a grimace or a frightening smile on its expression. He quickly stood up, being sure not to touch the thing that had crept up upon him unawares. He grabbed his weapons and beat a hasty retreat away from this place of his own vulnerability.

Savage was almost out of sight of the tree he had rested under when a thought came to him, *What worldly power stopped this monster from harming me?*

The bowman instantly knew what happened. He hastened back to the copper beech tree where he had rested, received aid and was protected from the wrath of perdition.

Underneath the Sentinel Tree that had harbored him safely, he knelt down on the ground alongside Ünger. He said aloud,

"Oh God above, mighty in puissance and percipience art Thou.

Thy power and Thy perception have sought and found me.

Because of your divine love for me you have protected my spirit, my soul and my body from this horrid evil from Abaddon.

I thank thee for your love and grace. May my sins be shriven.

May my family and King be protected.

May those under my care be watched and guided by the same hand that oversees and watches over me.

May my steps be taken safely and with blessing upon your path.

If perchance, I stumble, may I be lifted onto my feet once more; May I serve without failure and fault until the end of my days."

Without looking at Ünger, Savage walked gently toward the tree. He placed his hand on the copper beech and said, "Thank you, O Mighty One, for listening to our Creator and protecting me thus from such repugnance."

Setting his weapons in place upon his body, he retraced his steps to the farmstead.

The bowman decided to approach the farmstead frontally. Thus he entered the farm from the wagon road. He proceeded with extreme caution into the late farmer's land and possessions. He carefully assessed if there was any evidence of the other two Üngers, its divisions, or even if the one underneath the Sentinel Tree had somehow revived, and raced ahead of him to the farm.

Ünger, he thought, *is a crafty beast. He might be skulking anywhere behind, or attempt flanking, me.*

Savage checked for the presence of any human or other sentient creature. He went through the house, barn and other outbuildings. He walked the farmland once. Nothing living, except for himself, was found. The place was deserted even by animals, birds and insects. Deflated, empty bodies of twenty-six Marauders, not including the farmer and his family who still remained in the barn loft, were found in various places where they were consumed by Ünger and his partitioned selves. The chill feeling of dread saturated everything around the property.

He returned to the privy next to the barn and followed the erratic tracks made by Error as he escaped from the outhouse. The human scat that the Captain left behind, along with his footprints, revealed that he had run at various speeds. It also showed to the trained eye of the big man that Error had zigzagged back and forth in a five to fifteen foot wide path. Toward the end of this particular direction that he had gone in, the Captain had shuffled backwards for about another thirty feet.

Savage calculated that Error had gone in the opposite direction away from the main entrance to the farm for about two hundred feet before he came to an abrupt halt. The archer could see that the other man had stood there for a while. From the point where the green man had come to a full stop, Error retraced his steps, in a roughly parallel fashion, back to the barn, and then passed outside the farmstead itself.

Dissatisfied with what he had not found, Savage went back to the main house. He tallied in his mind again the dead he had seen. He realized that he had not found Mordant's body. The bowman laid out a series of imaginary grids around the farmhouse and proceeded to check them thoroughly. He was still patiently searching in the fourth grid when he came upon the boot marks of a man walking hastily in freshly tilled soil toward the forest.

The big man smiled grimly. With renewed determination he followed Mordant's track across the newly ploughed field into the woods.

Savage spent the next three days tracking Gregor Mordant. The archer began to realize that Mordant was not just trying to escape the dangers of the farmstead, but that he was on a course to go to the nearest village. The stream where Savage first met Pall turned into a river. At the point that it did so, a village had sprung on its banks. Here, the stream was now called the Forgotten River.

The bowman surmised that with Mordant's connections and ability to attain finances, the village was the most likely place for him to reach. From there he could gain passage on a small boat to go further downstream to the port city of Seascale. Or, if nothing was available for Mordant to travel on the river, he could purchase a horse and head down the road in the same direction.

Nothing to prevent me from trying the same thing, he said to himself.

Gullswater was a small town. It was close in vicinity, about forty miles, to one of the largest cities in this part of the country. Savage knew that once Mordant arrived in Seascale, he would be almost impossible to find. The window of his presence there would be very brief. The bowman knew that Gregor would find a ship passage almost forthwith. Once on board ship, Savage would not be able to apprehend him, let alone start interrogating the man for what he knew.

The bowman spent a brief moment eating the remaining food that he had left to him. The day before, in the late afternoon, while he had picked up his speed in following Mordant, a bevy of quail had exploded in flight directly underneath his feet. Quicker than thought, and with hunger facilitating his accuracy, he shot down three of the birds. He had cleaned, gutted and cooked them on the spot. He ate one and saved the other two for the following day.

The archer made the decision that he would now travel nonstop to Gullswater. The moon, which was waning gibbous, would still be bright enough at night for him to see clearly enough to make his way to the town.

Setting out again more swiftly than before having his all too sparse feast, his long even strides quickly covered a large distance. He came out of the forest while there was still a good bit of daylight left. He had entered a vast track of open grassland, meadows and tilled fields. No one could be seen for miles around.

I would have thought there might be evidence of the ravages of war here, he reflected to himself. He saw neither scouts on foot nor mounted outliers. Neither was there evidence of any victualers or sutlers, nor moving herds of animals to help feed the mouths of an army's hungry soldiers.

It was dusk when he reached the main road to Gullswater.

CHAPTER SIXTEEN

Mordant, having escaped the depredations of Ünger near the farmhouse and its surrounding buildings, crossed safely over a newly ploughed and hoed field. His men, in the meantime, were obviously not as fortunate because they were being relentlessly brought down by nine partitions of the beast.

He gained entrance to the forest without incident.

Reaching the edge of the trees, the Commander quickly enfolded himself into its depths.

After a while, he paused hesitantly in his flight away from the site of the slaughter. He gathered his thoughts together. Mordant became determined to get to Gullswater, to which he had assigned Error to reach earlier that evening, especially for the express purpose of getting in touch with their allies.

Soon enough, he arrived in the town and found himself at the riverside in front of a well neglected shack. Its corners stood out at odd angles. He knew that nothing was plumb in the structure whatsoever. The building leaned over towards the direction of the river in front of it.

It looks like a young wastrel. Nay, it's more like an old libertine gone into his cups and now hunches himself over ready to puke his guts out in the water.

The dwelling belonged to his chief of intelligence. Many residents of the town thought its owner was a recluse. Despite his outward appearance, Moro Asutuo was aptly named. His enemies called him the dark one, a cognomen or nickname that was quite apt. He had an acerbic disposition sometimes accompanied with a biting and wry sense of humor. Some, like Gregor Mordant, thought him brilliant, as his surname indicated. The hovel in which the Commander stood next to had become the center of his northeastern intelligence network. Asutuo's information was eerily reliable.

It was uncanny how Moro was able to discern the substance of a problem, be it one of supply, or one to be negotiated. Give him a human or political enigma and he could immediately see into the heart of it. It did not matter whether the issue dealt with royalty, clerics, landowners, or illicit lovers. Moro would configure the outcome in an uncanny, often fatalistic, way. Mordant had to keep the dark one leashed closely to him when it came to political intrigue between kings, fiefdoms, states and nations.

The Commander approached the shack and knocked on the top half of the broken front door. Initially, he stood still while appearing to be ready for someone to respond attentively to his presence there. When no one answered his rapped summons, Mordant shifted his position, almost looking as though he had given up on finding anyone present. Still standing in front of the door, he had moved to its far left, meanwhile stepping on a small piece of charcoal with the sole of his left foot. Shuffling his boot three times, as if he were waiting impatiently, he left a small X on the granite threshold.

Gregor waited there at the door for another forty heartbeats. He left looking somewhat disconsolate. Had others been following him, they would have seen that this particular visitor was now thirsty and desirous of a hot meal and drink to wash it down. Their steps would also have taken them to the Gullswater Tavern, which was a destination he quickly reached.

It was at the point of Mordant almost finishing his meal when he felt the presence of the dark one seated two tables over on his right. Seemingly ignoring Moro's presence there, the Commander finished his food, being sure to smack his lips and show great delight in the Tavern's cuisine.

When the server came to take his plate away, Mordant ordered another drink for himself, "as well as for the gentleman all alone at the table on my right."

Mordant finished his drink and paid for his meal. He summarily left the place, after nodding briefly at Moro, who seemed to be nursing his ale with studied thought.

It was getting dark outside. The Commander took a slow, circuitous walk back to the disgruntled looking building. With the moon just past being full, darkness had come at last. He again approached Moro's place, using the light of the moon to guide him there. This time, however, Mordant went alongside the river and entered the building on the side facing the water.

The Commander stepped into an unlighted room. Soon, the creak of a door sounded, and a dull, flickering light outlined the partial opening of a door. He walked through and saw Moro seated at a cluttered table. To his left was a small stub of a candle, whose remaining amount of wax in its stand looked virtually negligible.

"Buona sera, Patron," greeted Moro.

"Buona sera, Capo," returned Mordant.

Asutuo blew out the candle. Moonlight flooded into the room. The man turned and proceeded to walk out of the building. The Commander followed his chief to a small skiff, which was tied off and moored to a small pier on the river.

Mordant climbed into the boat and sat down in the bow.

Moro clambered in lithely. He stepped into the stern. While the dark one released the stern line, Mordant did the same with the one near him. Both men made sure the spring lines were cleared as well. Situating himself expertly in the middle of the boat, Moro placed an oaken oar in each hand. He quietly and capably rowed the small craft to a place further upstream just out of sight and a good stone's throw past his own place of disrepair.

Upon reaching their destination, they did the reverse of their tending to the craft at the beginning of their brief voyage by mooring it securely to the iron cleats on another small pier.

They walked up a graveled path that led to Moro's home. Once inside, Moro went to a banked fire in a small hearth in his kitchen area. He took a compact, handheld bellows and provided a whoosh of air into the banked coals. Soon a fire warmed the room. The chief beckoned his commander to make himself at home and to sit in one of the five chairs placed at an eating table.

Once both men were seated, Moro said, "I have taken measures, Commander, to provide you with passage on a larger boat to Seascale."

"Grazie, Capo."

"Non parlarne, il meo Comandante," purred the dark man reassuringly.

The Commander sat back while his chief of intelligence served them both a drink of wine. He watched Moro closely. "It should not do so by now, my friend," he said, "but your perception is the greatest charm you have, and it still surprises me."

"It is what I was given and use in your service, Commander."

"Yes, Moro, it is a gift and deeply appreciated."

"Your offer of praise and thanks are welcome," Asutuo answered, then added, "We will rise at dawn."

Without any further discussion, they finished their drinks. Moro bid his commander a good night. He left the room and went to get his rest for the evening.

Mordant got up from the table and walked into an adjoining room where there was a cot. He flung himself upon it and soon joined his chief in sleep.

At dawn, Moro woke his commander. They left the house and walked back down the gravel path to the small boat. Moored next to it was a longboat waiting to take the Commander downstream.

A large, heavily bearded man came to the side of the boat to offer the Commander his arm. As Mordant boarded this larger vessel, Moro introduced him to the captain of the boat, saying, "Captain Eumero will take good care of you, Sir."

"I am sure of it, Capo," Mordant said softly.

The Commander stepped amidships, being sure not to interfere with the working of the Captain and his crew, who were preparing to get the longboat moving into the center of the river.

No further words were exchanged between Moro and Mordant.

The dark one raised his left hand slightly in farewell as the longboat moved away from its mooring. As he did so, he said softly, "Può potere sopraffare i tuoi nemici."

Eumero, who was used to Moro's intoned farewell, smiled upon hearing it, and stated, "May power not only overwhelm our enemies, Capo, but lead to their utter desolation."

The dark one grimaced, rather than smiled.

He remained standing on the side of the bank, watching the longboat be drawn downriver.

When Moro's place had disappeared from view, the Captain came over to Mordant. They shook hands peremptorily.

"Benvenuto a bordo *La Signora Maria*, tuo Onore," The Commander looked steadily at the man.

Somewhat uncomfortable with Mordant's neutral expression, Eumero unnecessarily gave the translation of his previous greeting, saying, "Welcome aboard my longboat, *The Lady Mary*, Your Honor."

"Thank you, Captain."

"She's a good boat, Sir," came the assurance of the craft's merit from her captain. "She's built in the clinker style. Her planks are hung overlapped on a frame. She can carry more weight and more cargo than a ship bigger than her built carvel style."

The Commander nodded his head to this information.

Eumero continued with a belated explanation, "Some shipwrights will tell you she's built with a lapstrake method."

"Such construction allows the boat to bear most of its load on the hull," Mordant said.

This time, the Captain looked surprised at the Commander's statement.

"She's built like a raider," Mordant elucidated, "She can carry a bigger cargo because the frame is built stronger per its unit weight. The only drawback to its style of configuration is that a bigger vessel of its kind poses a risk in eventually having its planks split along the nail or spike holes."

Captain Eumero laughed good naturedly, "I can see you're a man who knows his way around a vessel."

"Thank you, Captain."

"Please make yourself comfortable, Your Honor. We will soon arrive safely at the port city of Seascale."

Eumero strode back over to his helmsman and started a conversation with him.

Mordant walked leisurely to the bow of the boat. He watched the wake it was making for a little while. It seemed to soothe his spirit. He sat down under the longboat's figurehead. His head nodded on his chest.

The Lady Mary, with its captain, crew and a sleeping commander, all too soon passed from view on that part of the Forgotten River.

Later on that morning, Savage arrived in Gullswater. He did not find Mordant there.

CHAPTER SEVENTEEN

Pall had stepped on the roots of the copper beech tree that were right next to its base. Doing so placed his face closer to the silvered hide of the hardwood tree. Even though he tried not thinking in order to protect himself from being detected by Ünger, his mind made the association of the word *hardwood* with Meginhard.

Unbidden, at least consciously, he went back in time to the culminating test ruthlessly given to him and his fellow recruits at the end of his second round of basic training with the Aeonian Guard.

They were placed in a large combat training field. There was no grass, only a whitish, sandy soil that raised a cloying dust in thick clouds whenever any form of combat practice was held. All nine recruits were in line standing at attention. Arrayed outwards from them were the Aeonians themselves. Archers were placed on ten–foot stands around them to make sure no escape was to be made on anyone's part. These bowmen were also there to ensure justice was meted out to the recruits if any, some or all failed the sentence, or challenge, Pall had given the High Marshall upon the young man's killing of the giant Savaric.

Umbré was given pride of place and was seated in a set of stands made for review purposes of the combat practice occurring on the field. Captain Martains stood by his right side.

Sergeants Meginhard and Burchard stood in front of the nine recruits.

At a given point, when almost four hundred men were assembled together on the field, the Marshall slightly nodded to his captain. Martains waved his right hand for the tests to begin.

Sergeant Burchard called the recruits' roll. Starting with the spokesman of the group first, he called out in a loud voice that clearly was heard by every man in attendance.

Jarin de Ashton
Ector Collier
Thurstan Gage
Brom Hovey
Samar Jackson
Adam Underhill
William Victor
Pall Warren
Rulf the Younger

Upon hearing their respective name called, each recruit stepped forward and gave a sharp assent of, "Present."

Sergeant Burchard proceeded to separate the recruits into a semi–circle by having them stand twenty–five feet apart from one another.

When this task was completed, Captain Martains ordered their opponents to come forward.

Thirty–six, well chiseled and powerful men, ready for death by combat, emerged from the right of the Aeonian ranks.

Another dozen of like caliber soldiers moved in from the left side. The recruits were not surprised. They knew Sergeant Meginhard was determined to ruin them.

Except for the wind occasionally sending small twisters of dust around them, silence reigned supreme while these veterans were getting in their own lines of order. When their swift movement was completed, there were four rows of twelve Aeonians in each line arrayed in front of the nine recruits.

Every elite fighter carried his own weapon of choice, as well as a sword and a brace of knives to go with each veteran's own blade. Some had kite-shaped shields, straight and curved, or triangular designed, strapped onto their arms. As a group of warriors, they were evenly divided between dominant left and right hand fighters.

Broadswords, claymores and longswords predominated for long bladed weapons. They were either sheathed in a scabbard on the fighters' side opposite their preferred hands, or strapped in place on their backs.

Flanged maces, morning stars, two war hammers and a flail were held loosely in some of the respective fighters' hands, ready to be wielded against the young men.

A variety of axes were carried by the veterans. These weapons ranged from a battle wagoner's to various throwing axes. One warrior carried a vicious looking mattock made especially for close combat.

An assortment of spears and polearms were also being hefted with expert familiarity.

When all four dozen of them were assembled in line, Captain Martains addressed the command staff, combatants, surrounding archers and veterans on the field:

"We are here today to do trial by combat.

The sentence as requested and given to the High Marshall by recruit Pall Warren upon the death of our comrade Savaric was accepted in the place of the corporal's death.

We stand before everyone present here this

187

morning to witness what was ordained by command. Any recruit who survives the trial enters with full honors into the Aeonian Guard.

Those who fail die, their heads are cut off and thrown in a separate place away from their bodies. The victors are those predestined and blessed by the just and good Lord above as rightful champions. Our unit, is the most decorated and esteemed in the King's armies. It is one in which each man here has fulfilled and reached the apex of his strength, honor, courage and knowledge of the arms he bears so well.

The motto of our force is *Si vis pacem, para bellum*, Given by Vegetius, it is one for which we live daily: 'If you want peace, prepare for war...'
This day, we await the justice about to be attained.

This contest is to the death."

A huge roar of approval thundered across the field. The Aeonian lust for fatal damage to rain down on the nine recruits before them was as visible as the sun overhead.

The sergeants first placed four veteran warriors apiece in strategic positions in opposition to each recruit. Following this arrangement, Burchard assigned one more veteran to each recruit, excluding Pall. Meginhard then took the remaining three elite warriors, and with a satisfyingly evil grin on his dour face, put them around Pall.

High Marshall Solace Umbré stood up from where he was ceremonially seated on a battlefield chair. Taking an eight–foot, Angon javelin from his spearman, who was standing to his left, the Marshall threw it with expert force just before the place where Jarin de Ashton, the spokesman for the young companions, stood at attention.

When this throw was completed and the spear was quivering in the dirt disturbed ground, forty-eight men rushed nine.

Before the dust obscured their vision, hand signals flew rapidly from the young spokesman's free hand to his comrades as the Aeonians charged the recruits. Jarin retracted the javelin from where its tip had penetrated on the practice field. To the surprise of everyone present, and with all eight shields up in place, the arc in which Sergeant Burchard put the young men collapsed into a small, compact square.

A clamor of surprise was sent rebounding across the field from the collective Aeonian throat.

The elite guards charging the young recruits grunted en masse as they burst upon, and attempted to overwhelm, the square of armed men in front of them. All forty–eight warriors could not be up against the square in front of them simultaneously. The geometry worked against them as they ground into the recruits' upheld shields.

Blood started flowing. It was mostly Aeonian.

In the center of the square, a young man, heretofore thought unfortunately lucky when pitted against Savaric, turned into a killing machine.

No one, except for the High Marshall himself, had ever seen a man fight in the manner and prowess being displayed before them.

In the blink of an eye, seven men were dispatched efficiently by the eight holding the square in place. Warren killed another five and severely handicapped another three by chopping off three arms belonging to their respective owner's bodies. His sword had penetrated another warrior's cuirass and stuck there. When the man mortally fell, he was out of reach so that Pall could not retrieve his sword.

Taking advantage of another's weakness upon dying, Pall wrested the man's pike away from him. The young warrior now had the use of a long thrusting spear that he could wield with both his hands. Employed with great effect against cavalry assaults, its fourteen–foot length was a perfect weapon to have in close order combat in this formation.

The men in the square killed another four Aeonians before Pall settled down with the pike in his hands.

The veterans raging against the eight–shield wall were far from being novices in battle. A great hatred was fiercely churning in their guts against these young, insolent boy soldiers. These Aeonians began to adjust to the square and started taking turns in attacking it. Some actually were smiling at the thought they had turned the momentum against the young companions. One front line of men, comprising six men on each side, exchanged places with another line. The three remaining veteran elite stood outside the battle proper acting as guides to help their compatriots charge the square in the best possible manner. The men inside the square neither could rest nor best adjudicate their combat strategy. They were eventually going to be defeated by enervation and brute strength massed against them.

Another two veterans were knocked out of the contest.

However, Ector, Thurstan and Rulf had received egregious damage to themselves. The heavier weapons used against them were taking grim effect. Adam was noticeably limping badly from receiving a crushing blow from one of the flanged maces that landed just above his upper left knee.

The men in line directly against the companions were replaced by the men in line behind them. Pall instantly decided to take advantage of this exchange when it next occurred. When the transfer of Aeonian warriors occurred, he shouted the word, "Spiral!"

Heedless of the punishment they were receiving, the veteran onlookers were treated to the sight of a battle square of eight men inexorably revolving around its center.

The Aeonian audience also was treated chillingly to a man now gone berserk, but who still remained a rational weapon of destruction unto himself. He had dispatched, in close order, three men, and another three, before his pike was broken in two by the warrior using the last war hammer left to the veterans remaining standing.

An additional three soldiers, one being the soldier handling the war hammer, were disabled by those holding the square in place.

Sixteen very distraught and surpassingly angry veterans remained in the fight.

Before the square collapsed from the mortal injuries taken by Ector, Thurstan and Rulf, Brom had managed to retrieve Pall's falchion sword. As Brom handed it back to him, Jarin yelled, "Devolve!"

Almost instantly, upon hearing his order, five companions stood in an arc again with the weaker four in line behind them.

Ector, Thurstan and Rulf were lying in separate pools of blood, slowly dying. Adam's leg being so heavily crushed, leaned fully upon his shield.

Combat between both sides suddenly halted and was broken off.

Men, although not wanting to do so, had to rest from their exertions against and with one another.

The Aeonian audience looked on sullenly. A dawning admiration for what the young recruits were accomplishing was beginning to take place in many of the veterans' estimation of the skills of combat being displayed before them.

Pall stood in the center of the arc. He did not seem to be tired at all.

The dust had not yet begun to settle back on the practice ground when, "This young bitch needs to be taught a lesson," was screamed by one of the veteran adversaries at Pall. The man had withdrawn the javelin Jarin had used at the inception of the combat from the body of a fellow warrior. Fully incensed, he ran toward Pall and threw it at him with admirable speed and deadly force.

William, also now seriously hurt, still managed to deflect it away from Pall by sweeping his shield underneath the flight of the javelin.

Ricocheting off the force of the shield, the spear flew into the command staff area.

It struck the right side of Captain Martains chest armor as he stepped in front of the Marshall to protect him from it. The power of the violence placed into the throw by the avenging veteran became increased even more when the top part of William's shield hit underneath the first quarter of the spear. When both objects came in contact with each other under these conditions, the javelin truly became a lethal missile. The point punctured the captain's armor and penetrated into his right lung.

A collective sigh went up out of everyone's throats, including the remaining combatants on the practice field. The man who made the throw acted as if he had received a mortal stroke as well. He dropped his arms and shoulders in defeat and put his left hand over his face.

Combat on the practice field stopped permanently.

The archers positioned on their stands un–nocked their bows and stood down from their places.

Men crowded around the Captain, the command staff and the stand upon which they were assembled.

Sergeants Meginhard and Burchard tried to give the fatally wounded captain some room. No one moved or listened to their protestations to the contrary.

The High Marshall, with tears falling slowly onto his beard, knelt down and placed his captain's head on his lap.

Men on the outside started moving away from someone approaching the stand.

Pall moved as if in a dream. The two–edged, falchion sword was still in his grip. He was bloody from wounds received on the field. He was dripping from the spatter and gore of battle.

He reached the inner circle unmolested and then stood before the kneeling Marshall Umbré and the prone position of Captain Martains.

The Marshall looked a silent question at Pall. Officers moved out of the way as the young man came close to the center of this tragic panorama.

Pall knelt down alongside the Captain. He placed the falchion sword on top of the dying man and held it in place with his left hand.

He asked the Marshall's spearman to withdraw the Angon javelin from the Captain's injured and wrecked chest.

The spearman refused to do it because he knew that this type of weapon was by design, difficult, if not impossible, to remove from wood let alone flesh.

Wrapping his hands firmly around the haft of the javelin, Pall removed the spear as easily as if he were taking a knife out of heated cheese.

He knelt back down over the Captain's form. At first, Pall's eyes focused on the distant horizon. Dust devils sprang up around the reviewing stand. He looked up at the heavens above him. The young man raised his right arm and with palm lifted toward the sky above him, he closed his eyes and sang a prayer of healing:

"A fool has failed again in the feebleness of his
   effort.
To do what is merciful and righteous in the eyes
   of the
Lord is but a mere beginning step on His path, His
Desire for us to walk with Him and in His love for
   us.

O Lord of Armies, I am but a buffoon, a mere whiff
Of smoke that once appearing in the air of this
   realm,
Disappears instantly and forever; I am here only in
The blink of time's moment, while you, O God, are
Time's Creator—You are Eternal and Constant.

It was you who set the worlds in motion. You who
Placed the sun, the moon and the very ground
Underneath my feet in their places upon the deep
   waters;
I ask that the fountain of your love burst forth like
   springs
Filled with the living power of compassion and
   kindness.
I seek Thy hand, asking that you favor the
   contrition of my
Soul. This blade which I place on this mortal man
   is made
By the hands, skill and genius of my father's love. The

Blade is made from the steel of heaven itself. It is
   crafted in
Penance, prayer, songs and the reciting of psalms
   to become
An instrument of protection for the weak, ill and
   aged.

I beg you humbly to heal this worthy captain
   before you;
I offer a petition to you that this great sword on
   his body
Be now wielded by your Spirit as a fearsome
   balm of
Healing. May he rise whole again. May he be of true
Service to your cause, as well as to the King and
   to the
Living in this hallowed land."

In soaring melody, Pall intoned this prayer twice.
During the time it was sung, utter stillness overcame
and drenched the field and people with its potency.
Men, grown satirical, proud and selfish, bowed their
heads and wept silently to themselves. Men who
doubted that a divinity ruled and cared for the
living, opened their hearts to entertaining the truth
of such a verity. Some who had grown callous of
life's suffering, remained so even more, but their
eyes and hearts opened to what they saw happening

around them. Those, complacent in their daily lives, now questioned the worth of such a conceit.

The deep pallor and purple hue affixed to the Captain's features gradually lifted away from him. His labored breathing evened out and slowed to a more healthy rhythm. The blood pulsing out of the puncture hole made by the javelin, decreased, came to an end and ceased altogether.

Men's wounds—who were still in the land of the living—from the battle just waged in front of the Aeonian elite, stopped bleeding, closed themselves and healed over.

Then dread, indeed, fell upon the warriors in this field: For these fierce, proud men had met the God of Armies, firsthand.

Pall stopped singing.

He opened his eyes and saw the Captain's clouded grey eyes steadily looking at his own blue pair. The two men smiled at one another and laughed deeply at the joy still left in creation around them.

CHAPTER EIGHTEEN

Pall opened his eyes at the sound of laughter. For a space of time, he was confused over his whereabouts.

He felt a sense of vertigo and thought, *Am I back in the square with my brothers revolving it around me?*

Yet, there were no weapons in his hands and he did not feel the heat of battle upon him. Pall could not get a sense of equilibrium back into himself. He felt as though reality had collapsed on him.

Does Ünger have the power to suck out the presence of this world like he empties out the bodies of men? he asked himself in alarm.

He started to realize that he was standing on the roots of a very old Sentinel Tree. In a rush of remembrance, he understood that he was near the majestic tree because he was hiding from Ünger.

He opened his physical senses to his surroundings. The wind soughed gently through the leaves in the copper beech. He heard the same sound of wind caressing the leaves in the other trees nearby him as well. It reminded him of a tide coming in and out of an ocean pool.

Some birds called to one another, flew over him and landed in the branches far above him. Sunlight reached into the depths of the Sentinel Tree and burnished the copper and purple leaves until he thought the very color shining from them was in a flame of its own making.

Pall cautiously looked around him. Seeing nothing to fear, he stepped away from the tree and looked on the other side that was previously hidden from his view. Again, nothing alarming was to be seen, heard, tasted or smelled. He decided that there was no corruption from Ünger's touch in this part of the woods.

He shook his head as if a fit of fever had overcome and suddenly left him. He began to relax the state of hypervigilance he had been keeping. His heart rate settled back to normal. His breathing calmed down.

The young man smiled because he had more puzzles to consider. *What happened to Ünger? Did he just go away? Did he attack Error?*

Pondering these matters to himself more, he returned to the place where he had stood next to the copper beech when the encounter with Error and Ünger materialized as if it were a disturbing dream.

"A nightmare, truly," he considered softly aloud to himself.

Pall gathered his few belongings together, then paused in placing them on his person.

I made a mistake in looking upon these true gifts as meager. I am richly endowed with offerings priceless in their merit to me.

Except for his sword, he placed everything that he had just taken in hand back against the Sentinel Tree. Standing a comfortable distance away from its trunk, he drew the blade completely from its sheath. As Pall looked at the strange glistening metal he held in front of him, he thought more deeply about its making.

He thought about his father and what he now could recall about him. Certainly, he was a mighty warrior who commanded all of the King's armies at one time. His knowledge about men, war and leadership was something he stood in awe about, especially considering his father did not seem to carry the weight of it as a burden. His expertise and accomplishments in arms and the making of weapons seemed to more than rival that of anyone else in high command.

Add all of these qualities to his piety, as well as his love for his family, home and craft, and you have a redoubtable and unique man.

"But my father," he said to the tree next to him, "seemed so filled with peace. I could always talk with him, and was eager so to do."

The young man paused, as if waiting for the tree to respond to his musing.

He looked up high into its branches where he could see it moving in time with the wind's rhythm.

"He poured all of himself into making this glaive. I remember now that he said to me: *Son, there is a vein of corruption in human beings. Whatever they touch is tainted with this ill nature. This falchion sword was made for the purpose of combating such evil. It was made to fulfill the purpose of peace."*

Pall became silent. He listened to the sounds of nature going on around him. "I served as apprentice at the forge, and in learning the art of fighting, to a man who was my father," he wondered aloud with awe.

"Yet this sword, so simple, elegant and sure, was made for me with a metal mixed from one of heaven's own starry host. My mother and da told me that they could not send me away from them caparisoned with a noble's mien. It would have brought false attention to me, and perhaps I would have become an ill-omened challenge to those I encountered. I probably would have puffed myself up and become a strutting, disgusting peacock."

He fell silent once more.

He looked at the copper beech tree and held the sword high in salute to it. "I plight this pledge to you, O Sentinel of the Wood: I will spend my time, until my promise is met, learning the nature of this sword. I will use it for the purpose it was made. I will grow like you and be a boon to all those who seek safety within the sweep of my arm."

The growing and greater awareness he was attaining about who he was and what he had been through, helped steady the inner core of his heart. "Even though there is a vast amount I still do not know about myself, I have faith it will return to me," he said.

"If I get in trouble, or need some help, I will return to you," he said to the majestic tree before him. With mocking, but understated humility, he added, "Or, if I have your liege's pardon, I will avaunt myself to one of your brothers to seek his council fair."

A gust of wind rushed into the base of the tree's canopy and moved the tree into a rhythm of affirmation to Pall's statement and mood.

The young man laughed again, as he and Martains did on the morning of the Captain's miraculous healing.

Pall sheathed the bright sword in its rightful scabbard. He picked up his other belongings and walked down the path to where it intersected with the road from which Merek and he flew in alarm.

Pall reheard Savage telling him where to meet the bowman. His decision made, the young warrior walked back down the wagon road. He was looking forward to seeing the archer once more. He wanted to share with Savage the hopes Pall had in attaining the full potential and promise that the God of Armies had for him.

The young warrior brought to mind the directions Savage had given in order to meet up again with the archer. Merek was with him then. Pall wondered what happened to him, if he was alive and safe after their flight from the dreaded Ünger. The young swordsman keenly felt the loss of Carac. Time had run out for Carac, cruelly so. Pall wondered why some men died, or some were injured and disfigured horribly from accidents or combat, while others survived. Was it God's hand that made such a determination of fate?

Is man destined to a preordained end? Or, are we just pawns in a game between powers we can only surmise are present, and that faintly?

He sensed battle memories surging for release deeply within him. Faint images arose like shadows cast on a wall in a cave from the light of a fire. Men on horses circling a phalanx of armed pike men; two champions fighting for victory with the armed might of two hosts waiting petulantly for the outcome; men falling in the mire and bloody gruel of combat in an early morning deluge of rain and arrows....

All round him, the great scythe of death reaped its eager and grim toll. Friend and foe, ally and enemy, collapsed, were torn apart, disappeared in a spray of blood. The wonder and guilt of it all were seen in the survivors who walked away from the sufferings of war.

Pall shook his head as if to dislodge his melancholy through such a physical gesture. Too much time had gone by since he last saw the big man. Savage had advised to keep walking on the road if he had not been able to meet Pall and Merek.

The young man decided to keep on the road in the direction he was heading. "I wonder where it will lead me?" he asked himself aloud.

He walked until it started becoming dark. For most of the time he was alone. He had only seen two groups of people pass by him as they were traveling in the opposite direction in which he was bound. The first group consisted of an extended family fleeing from the area. They were in several wagons that were respectively pulled by horses and oxen. Husbands and wives, children and the aged, were huddled together on the road. Frequently looking behind them with alarm, they passed by him silently, looking at him with much suspicion and dread. They took account of his age and that he was dressed for war. Then, hurried by him with no salutation, but a deprecation or two muttered inarticulately under their collective breath.

The second group consisted of several armed men. They were escorting a herd of goats. Pall stepped off the road to let them pass. When these men came even with him, they nodded curtly, but without any rancor in their expressions. The oldest of them stopped and talked briefly with Pall.

"The road's washed out couple miles ahead. You'll have to swim across to get to the other side. Then again, you could hang back a bit, wait for the water to retreat back to its normal level."

"Thank you for your telling me, sir," Pall said to him politely.

"Least I can do for one of the King's own," the herder responded. "My father used to be one of the major victualers for his Highness when my da was a young man like you. He traveled with the monarch for twenty–five years."

"Thank you for your family's service to the Realm," said Pall.

The goat herder nodded his head in silent acknowledgment to Pall's homage.

"Keep your eyes sharp, young one," advised the old one. "You're headed to Gullswater. Not much there to recommend it except passage to Seascale."

Upon hearing this information, it was Pall's turn to nod silently.

The man smiled sadly, "Blessings to you. May your passage be a safe one."

"Thank you, sir. May your kind words return to you and yours fourfold."

Surprisingly, the man reached into his pack and brought out a carefully wrapped bundle. "Tis some dried goat meat jerky," he informed the young man. "It goes a long way. Use it sparingly."

Pall continued to stay off the road as he watched the herders and their goats pass by him. Eventually, they all disappeared from view as they went over a rise in the road. Before the old man walked over it, he waved a silent goodbye to Pall.

Pall walked to the point in the wagon road where it had been flooded over.

As it was almost dark, he decided to stop for the day. He determined to cross over to the other side of the road in the early morning. The young man walked directly off the road to his left. He went several hundred yards into a copse of alders and young poplar. Much of it was infested with briars. Worming his way carefully into the middle of this area, he reached a small clearing where he bedded down for the evening.

Pall was too tired to eat.

He thought of the kindness of strangers in the midst of war. He thought of the new found friends he had met during such trying times.

His mind drifted into rest.

He fell quickly and profoundly into the arms of sleep.

A smile remained on his countenance. Had it been light, one viewing him so would have thought that it softened his face well.

Pall slept deeply and soundly for most of the night. Halfway into the early morning hours, he awoke with a start. A dream of startling clarity had come to him. Yet, upon snapping out of sleep so suddenly, the memory of where he had been was yanked away from his ability to recall it.

The more he tried concentrating on what he had been dreaming about, the more lost it became to his mind.

It was something to do with a cliff overlooking the ocean, he pondered to himself. There was a clear sky, gulls calling to one another in high pitched cries.

"Maybe it was about when I reach Gullswater," he said out loud in the middle of the thicket.

But that's not right, either, because the old goat herder said that I could get passage to another place, Seascale.

"Gullswater's a stopping off place to a port city," he said aloud in response to his previous thought.

Savage could be in either place. *If I make the inquiries to the right people, they should be able to tell me whether or not they saw a seven-foot man walk by them.*

At last, he had talked himself out. The inner and outer conversations ceased. Closing his eyes once again, he fell asleep.

208

Pall awoke with the dawn light and the vision of a pair of hazel green eyes looking with alarm deeply into his. They were young eyes, a beautiful woman's, actually.

He thought, *I must have been thinking of my mother who gave birth to me.*

However, once this thought crossed his mind, he knew it was incorrect. Those stunningly clear pair of eyes belonged to another.

He sat up from the place of his evening's deep, but somewhat disturbing, rest. Remaining in place, he set out the rest of his food in front of him in a straight line. Cheese, a small variety of dried berries, fruit, nuts and goat jerky remained in his sparse, traveling larder.

He placed nine of these items in another line and rearranged the rest of the items of food around the nine. Before he knew it, he had the nine items in a "fighting square".

Pall inhaled a deep breath of air and froze in place. His mind went blank. For a moment he was back in the middle of the square with his friends, all fighting for their lives and for one another.

He forced the memory from him and stood up. When he bent over to pick up the food, he discovered that tears were rolling down his face.

He packed his food back into the case, *First obtained by Savage.*

Tears flooded from his eyes.

Given to a remorseful prison guard, Merek.

He had some trouble catching his breath. Sweat poured off him. His hands shook slightly as he put his belongings on him.

Who, in turn, passed it on to me.

Pall struggled back out of the coppice and practically jumped into the middle of a family that had pitched a temporary camp off of the wagon road where he had stepped away from it the night before.

The young family into which he had literally and physically jumped into had just been getting up and attending to feeding themselves. The husband was young and only a bit older than Pall. The man could have been an older brother in age to Pall. Upon Pall's bursting in on them, the "older" man alertly started for the wagon where he had taken out a quarterstaff.

Once the staff was in the man's possession, he charged Pall with it over his head in upraised position.

Pall immediately dropped to his knees. He looked briefly into the other man's eyes. He let go of this visual connection and cast his eyes to the ground, saying, "Prithee, I beg your most generous forgiveness for my clumsiness and error."

The man approached Pall and stopped eight feet away. Keeping the quarterstaff in the high, overhead strike position, he said, "You most certainly have my attention. Whether you are brigand, soldier or both, you have come upon us in a most unseemly and brazen fashion."

"I am but a pilgrim in this land and in this vale of time. I am a stranger to this land, and the land is a stranger to me."

The staff was lowered to a chest high thrust, if it was necessary to make one. "Aye, and you are but passing strange to me and my family's eyes."

Two little girls, twins, came out from behind the wagon. Their mother trailed close behind them, trying to catch them. They ran up to Pall. Standing directly in front of him, they said, "Papa, look we have company!"

The staff was quickly reversed in the man's hands. The lower end was raised off the ground two feet and stayed steadily to the left of the man's left foot. The staff was arranged diagonally to his body with the upper end over his right shoulder.

The mother tried gathering her daughters together back into her arms.

They easily skipped away and danced around the young man who remained kneeling in front of them.

"Good Pilgrim," one of them addressed Pall, "Why are briars sticking onto your arse and back? The other little one started to giggle.

Both girls, laughing uproariously, broke away from the strange young man.

Pall's face turned a deep red out of embarrassment, as they ran over to their father, who seeing them in such lively spirits, placed his staff upright against his left shoulder.

He broke into a hearty laugh. "My name is Thomas Cooper. People call me Tom, though."

His wife had stood up and moved over to her husband.

"This fine woman is my wife Alicia."

Alicia briefly bowed her head upon her introduction.

"The two fearsome creatures that accosted you are our life and treasure: Myra and Mary."

"I am Pall, with a double L, Warren," announced the young man.

"I thought the man's name was Pilgrim, Da," said Myra.

"Perhaps it is so," enjoined Alicia, and spelled with a double L as well."

Everyone was smiling.

Tom commanded gently, "Please arise, fair Pall, and be welcome to our camp this early dawn day."

Pall stood up.

"I can see no danger or ill will in you," Alicia said. "Besides, if you were a threat to us, you would do better taking yon briars off your person."

Once more smiles and gentle laughter were exchanged.

"I must needs be on my best behavior for the sake of obeying the two small and wise oracles that have approached me this passing morn."

"Ma, what's a coracle?" asked Mary.

"An oracle, little one," laughed the father. "Hush now, leave Pall be and let's get our humble camp ready for breaking our fast for the night just waned."

Alicia extended both of her hands down and out to them. They took their mother's hands into their own and went with her to get food ready.

"I will be glad to refresh and restart the fire, if you wish, Tom," Pall said deferentially.

"Thank you, Pall. I would welcome your help."

Soon, the fire was going well, food was brought out, cooked, served and eaten.

Everyone fell into a rhythm of helping start the day with one another as though it was something they had done many times.

Pall helped Tom put the two large draft horses into their traces.

Seeing that Pall was familiar with the intricacies of getting a team into position, Tom began helping his wife with the final touches of making sure everything was back together and stowed securely in its rightful place.

213

When everything was in order and his wife and daughters were on the big wagon, Tom turned to Pall. "You are more than welcome to accompany us to Gullswater," he said.

"It will be an honor to do so, Tom. Thank you."

"Think nothing of it. The honor is just as much ours." The cooper paused, and then said, "Besides, you look a lot less formidable with the briars not sticking out of *your arse and back!*"

Both men smiled at one another.

Tom bent to the task of leading the horses to the edge of the stream. Alicia held the reins and expertly drove the big rig to that point.

They brought the wagon to the edge of the road where it was flooded by the water. They stood off about twenty feet from it.

Under normal conditions, the traveler would only have to ford a stream that was only two to three feet deep, perhaps four, in places. The scene that presented itself here was quite different. The water poured across the ford in a steady torrent downstream.

Tom signaled to Alicia to keep the brake on the wagon and to stay in place. He waved Pall on with him as they went to stand right before the water's edge.

"We need to see how deep and how fast the current truly is," he said to Pall.

Pall started to take his belongings off him. "I'll be glad to go in and see," he offered.

"Nay," responded the cooper, "let me try something drier for us."

Pall looked questionably at Tom.

"We're going to unhook Tom and Alicia here," he indicated to the two large horses in back of where the two young men stood.

"Mary and me named them that, Pilgrim," shouted Myra above them on the wagon's high positioned driver's seat.

"Hush, Myra," urged Alicia, "your da's working a solution out."

When both draft animals were free of their reins and their places in front of the wagon, Tom led them by their bridles to the edge of the road.

Referring to the horses, he said shyly and with a smile, "I'm going to ride Alicia. Tom will accompany Alicia and me for support. We'll see what we've got before us."

Pall nodded that he was okay with this arrangement.

Tom easily set himself in place upon the draft horse. He made a clicking noise and gently kicked the horse between her ribs and chest, urging her into the stream. Alicia instantly followed Tom's command. She gently walked into the water, while the other horse kept pace with her.

Pall watched as the water rose easily over Alicia's pastern, cannon bone, fetlock, knee and then forearm. Soon, her belly was in the water. Reaching her flank and then her croup in the water, she began swimming in powerful strokes. The water surged against horse and rider.

Shortly, all three were across the stream and onto the other side of the road.

Tom waved and helloed from the opposite side over to Pall.

Pall returned the greeting.

Tom quickly returned back over to his family and Pall's side of the road, with Tom the horse preceding them.

Riding up to Pall, Pall took the bridle and held the animal in place while Tom alighted back onto the ground.

"I'd say the depth," indicating the water he had just been in, "is at least eight to ten feet deep," Tom reported.

"How strongly was the water pulling at you?" Pall asked.

"Tolerable well," came the reply.

Alicia, hearing the two men speak plainly in front of her, asked her husband, "Can it be done, husband? Can we get across safely in the wagon?"

"Aye, I think so, lass. Let me ponder it a bit, though."

Pall looked at Tom. Without saying anything out loud, he thought, *I don't see how he's going to get them over that torrent in front of us.*

Tom could see the doubt in Pall's manner. He smiled briefly and stated forthrightly, "I can get us across if you lend us your help, Pall."

Pall nodded and said, "Well enough: tell me what I can do to be of aid to you and your family."

"Let's get Alicia and Tom back into their traces."

Both men put the large horses into place at the front of the wagon.

After this task was accomplished, Pall followed Tom to the back of the wagon. One end of a large canvas tarp, covering the wagon's unseen main cargo, was securely fastened to it.

Pall helped Tom take the canvas off, fold it and place it far enough from the stream onto dry ground. Ten well–constructed and large oaken barrels were left sitting in the open on the wagon.

Tom explained the procedure he had in mind. "We're going to empty everything we can off the wagon and keep it all here for a bit. If we tie off five of these barrels on each side of the wagon, it should help keep it afloat. Before we do that, all of us are going to take what wax I have and rub down the open parts of the wagon with it that will be exposed to the water."

All three adults bent to the tasks ahead of them, making sure that the girls stayed on the wagon.

After they had finished these first instructions, Tom said, "We'll place, for now, all our things onto the canvas. We'll, hopefully, come back for them on the horses once we get the wagon across the water. We can use some of the barrels again to help float our belongings across the stream with us.

I have a wealth of good hemp rope and two large sets of block and tackle. There are trees a plenty on the other side. One good one, especially, that I can secure one block and tackle to it. Same here on this side. Each horse will be on either side. Tom on the other end and Alicia here. They will help hold the ropes in place. If I feel it's not working, we'll have to build a couple of rafts to take the place of the barrels in floating the wagon across."

Everything in the wagon that was theirs was placed on the tarpaulin, including Pall's sword and scant possessions.

Tom and Pall moved the empty wagon, with the help of the horses Tom and Alicia, into the stream up to the middle of the ash hubs on the rear axle. One by one they secured the empty oak barrels onto both of the long sides of the wagon to cleats that were strategically placed there for tying off equipment.

They unhitched the team. Tom rode over to the other side of the road with a block and tackle. He secured it to the tree he had mentioned earlier in his instructions to them in getting the wagon across the flooded ford. He rode back and tied off the other end of the tackle to the front of the wagon. He did the same to the back end of the wagon, showing Pall what he was specifically doing.

"This way," Tom added, "we've got the wagon in hand in case the rush of the water wants to take her downstream."

The next step was to secure the rope to each horse. Alicia was assigned to pull the rope on the other side of the stream, while Tom stayed on the side where they all presently stood. Once Tom the horse was tied off with the block end, Cooper showed Pall how to stop the rope from moving in case it had to be done. "Any questions?" he asked.

Pall shook his head from side to side indicating he had none.

"When I'm ready, I'll give you a wave," informed Tom. "If anything happens, like the rope snapping in two, getting snagged or bound up—make sure you get away from it, especially the block," he smiled grimly. "Also, make sure you don't foul the coiled end of the rope. Don't get caught up in it if the rope gets away from you, too."

"Okay, Tom, understood."

Tom went over and hugged his wife and children.

"We'll be praying for you and Pall," said Mary.

"And we'll pray for the horses and the wagon, too, Da," added Myra.

Tom kneeled in front of both girls. "And I would like you to do that, my beautiful ones," he said to them after giving them both a hug and then a kiss on each of their foreheads.

When the horses and both men were set in their respective places, Tom waved his hand and shouted that he was going to start pulling the wagon across the ford.

Pall watched the front rope go taught and snap out of the water. With all of the slack in the line gone out of the rope, the wagon started slowly moving.

The water went over the hubs of the rear wheels, the spokes and the felloes as well. The barrels on the upstream side of the wagon, energetically bobbed up and down.

"She's floating!" excitedly yelled Pall.

Tom nodded his head.

The girls clapped their hands and shouted their approval. Before the wagon completely was immersed in the water, it pliantly seemed to follow the front rope's lead. It obediently went in a straight line directly heading toward Tom. However, once in the current, it awoke to the power of the water's sweep past the ford as it started to be pulled by it downstream. Its struggle to do so was checked by the ropes, which were in turn tied off to the trees and horses.

Tom started his horse in motion, playing out the rope and redirecting the wagon toward his direction.

Everything seemed to go the way it was intended to work. The wagon reached the beginning of the deepest part of the flooded road. Suddenly, it dipped into a chute of fast moving water. The ropes held but were strained to their utmost capacity to hold the wagon from being pulled downriver by the torrent pouring against it.

Pall felt the end of his rope become completely drawn tight. He heard a snap. The middle of the rope split asunder. Instantly, he heard it whine back at him.

Alicia screamed a warning.

The rope, moving violently through the air, sang its way toward him.

Pall gave the loudest warning shout to Tom that the young warrior could utter.

Instinctively, he jumped away from the rope. It whipped its way across the place in which he had been standing. The frayed end of the snapped rope whipped Pall in the right temple.

With the energy completely gone out of it, it fell in front of Tom the horse who looked at it quizzically. He brought his nose close to it, looked up at Alicia and the girls and snorted.

Tom had already seen and assessed what was happening to Pall.

To make up the loss of the drag rope, he made sure that he did not let any pressure off the lead rope. At the same time, Tom urged Alicia forward at a run and successfully drew the wagon across the deep end until it again stood on firm ground.

Tom released the rope off Alicia, jumped on her back and quickly crossed the stream over to Pall.

Pall never felt the snap of the rope hitting him. His attention was focused elsewhere.

He heard the flailing of large wings besides him. Something to his immediate left rattled out a guttural coughing. It soon switched to an oddly uttered laughter that was accompanied by a "toc–toc–toc–toc."

Pall also could make out the sound of a man coming out of a river. The man announced himself to the young man. "I am Herald," the being said.

He saw himself singing against a wattle fenced in area, as well as intoning a prayer in front of a man dying in the midst of a large band of warriors.

A voice cried out behind him, "Oh, brother, why doesn't the boy sing his prayer for...."

He felt completely disoriented. He looked down where he thought he was standing on his feet, but noticed, instead, he had fallen to the ground.

He shook his head in confusion.

Pall got back onto his feet. He realized with a start that he was no longer at the side of the flooded ford with Tom, Alicia and the girls.

Instead, he was in an armed camp.

The sun was high up in the noon sky. Gulls sounded overhead.

Men, fully armed for battle, were walking away from their tents in orderly fashion. Some were by themselves while the majority of soldiers were clustered together in informal groups. They were all heading toward the edge of a massive sward of land overlooking the Sea of Fáelán.

Out of curiosity, more than a sense of danger, he decided to follow them and to see where they were going.

It all felt very familiar to him.

I think I've been here before, he reflected silently.

Having time to look more closely at the manner of soldiers he was with and the design and style of their camp, colors and clothing, he concluded that he was definitely not in his own country anymore.

"I must be on the far coastal side of one of the Western Isles," he said aloud.

The soldiers next to him laughed.

One larger warrior buffeted Pall exuberantly on the young man's chest. "Aye, lad that was a right celebration. It took me a while to get my bearins this morning, too!" the soldier laughed generously. His companions laughed along with him.

Pall smiled indulgently at all of them. "Thanks for your understanding," he said to no one in particular.

"Hell's blood," derisively mocked another soldier walking in the group Pall had just joined.

Three or four soldiers yowled together at the same time. Most of the others laughed together with deep merriment at their howling.

"Why not join us on our way to the assembly?" asked the spirited warrior who first addressed Pall earlier.

Not saying anything in response, Pall nodded his head that he would walk with them.

"It's all right, boyo," an older man kindly said to him, "you'll get your legs back quick."

"Hey, Aldric," shouted another warrior to the one who first addressed Pall, "the lad here's without is arms!"

More laughter.

"Shush, now, men, can't ya see he's had a rough night,"

Aldric said while indicating with his hand that Pall was daft.

Some of the soldiers chuckled good–naturedly. Many just shook their heads in disbelief.

"It's all right, lad," Aldric told him. "We're just gonna ear what the beauty has to say to us. You'll be fine. Just stick with us. You'll soon get yer land legs goin again."

Pall did not even attempt to offer an explanation about his appearance.

He did not quite catch what Almaric, *Is that his name?* said. *They're going to hear about duty?*

Thankfully, no one else said something to Pall.

As the group of men Pall was accompanying marched loosely together up to the higher land, he could see that hundreds of others were doing the same thing.

Perhaps thousands, Pall thought.

Arriving at their destination, Pall saw that he was on a great height of land overlooking a crescent shaped bay upon which several hundred ships were anchored. In the middle of the field, a small dais had been built. From the distance where they had stopped to view the proceedings, Pall thought he could discern that the stand was made of stone. It shone brightly in the sun. It looked radiant, sparkling in places as though precious gems and minerals were set in its features.

No one was yet there standing on it. Soldiers of all ranks were still filing into the large field.

From the elevation where he was positioned, Pall could see part of the vast camp spread out around the promontory below.

The conversations around him were subdued. Men waited expectantly for what was going to take place before them.

Out of sight of the assembly, horns sounded from three directions. Their calls were without melody, just a clamor, an aggravated ululation, for attention to be paid to something about to be announced.

A long column of six hundred warriors, marching six abreast, appeared. They marched toward the dais and upon reaching it, cordoned it off.

The horns went silent. No one throughout the vast array of men standing there said anything aloud.

Pall started to feel the pangs of a full blown headache begin to blossom behind his eyes.

Another group of men approached the field. They were dressed in flowing robes and led by two tall warriors who were each carrying one end of a heraldic banner. Scattered throughout this procession were a colorful variety of flags, standards, pennons, gonfalons and guidons, all carried proudly by warriors as well.

When this official looking group reached the dais, a section of the cordoned off area of men around it parted to let them through. This latter group also circled the dais, forming an inside ring similar to the larger one.

Everyone stayed still once the inner circle around the dais had formed.

Pall listened to the flags snap in the wind.

He felt like he was going to vomit.

Aldric, noticing that Pall was not looking well, placed his hand reassuringly on Pall's left shoulder and patted it two or three times.

Between surges of faintness, Pall saw a wagon drawn by a single black stallion appear onto the field. Driving it was a very slight, white-haired ancient. Around him and the wagon walked fifteen men.

Pall heard someone next to him murmur, "It's the Rover Captain and his men; he was touched by the Others."

An old man walked next into the sight of those assembled on the field.

"The hermit Greatworth," Aldric murmured.

Next to the hermit paced three great wolves. Silver gray in color, they walked with dignity.

Many warriors on the field drew unconsciously back from the sight of these august animals.

Horns sounded again. This time they repeated a sustained phrase of ascending notes as in a round or canon like form.

A single individual appeared walking from the camp below toward the center of the field. She was preceded by a knight riding a white stallion. He carried a large banner whose design contained three golden crowns encircled in a field of deep blue. Emanating three hundred sixty degrees from the enclosed crowns toward the four ends of the flag were rays of lightning, all arrayed in red and golden strikes. Those at the compass points were larger, sturdier looking and stitched in brilliant argent.

At first, Pall thought this person was a young boy as his height was shorter than those who preceded him. He was dressed in armor similar to what Pall had been wearing when he had been in the Aeonian Guard. The boy wore a sword and he was braced with a pair of throwing knives.

The soldier standing next to Aldric took one long look at Pall, at the young boy walking alone toward the dais and then back at Pall. Aldric nudged the man sharply with his elbow and silently motioned him to be still.

The hermit sat on the ground before the dais. The wolves rested at his feet. Men made sure to keep their distance away from them.

The young boy was led onto the dais by a man and a woman who both wore silver crowns on their heads. When he was between them they sat down at the same time while the boy remained standing.

For some reason, Pall started walking toward them.

Aldric tried to grab Pall by the elbow to prevent him from moving forward.

Pall shrugged him off.

The boy looked over the crowd. He turned around to make sure he had all their attention on him.

Men let Pall by them. Many purposely looked at him and what he was wearing. Some nodded their heads at him in acknowledgement and respect for whom they thought he appeared to be to them.

Pall was two hundred feet from the dais when the young boy turned halfway back in his direction. The lad took off his helmet and handed it to one of the men below the stand. He did something to the back of his head and a long shock of red hair cascaded down the back of "his" waist. Glints of blonde hair shone amongst the red.

A sense of surprise and confusion went through him.

This was no mere boy, but a diminutive and exceedingly beautiful looking young woman.

She raised both hands to the sky and looked at it steadily.

A roar from the field erupted in a sustained battle cry.

Pall continued walking.

Fifty feet away, the eighteen–year–old woman lowered her face and arms to the men around her. She took out a shining silver sword from the scabbard on her left side and held it high.

The roar of men continued unabated all during this time. Pall stopped walking.

He was twenty feet away from her.

The wind stopped. Every flag went motionless.

The vast company of armed might hushed themselves as one.

She lowered the sword and pointed it right at him, while looking to her right side. "We will conquer those who have oppressed us for too long," she said in a voice that carried the full length and depth of the field.

She looked to her left. "We will seek out those who have fostered a poison to imprison our fair land."

Pall felt himself trembling slightly.

The woman lowered the sword tip to the floor of the dais. "We will root them out and restore righteousness to our country."

A powerful shock of recognition dawned on him.

She looked directly at Pall. Her eyes widened in surprise.

When their eyes connected with one another, Pall bent over doubled and threw up on the ground. Something happened to him at the shock of contact with her when their eyes beheld each other. Information of a kind that he could not identify spilled out of her mind into his.

In the middle of his being sick, he heard the crowd crying her name.

Evangel! Evangel! *Evangel....*

———<del>—</del>├─•

"Are you alright, Pall?"

No answer was made.

"Pall?"

A groan came out him.

"I think he's coming round," said a feminine voice.

Another groan, then he dry heaved.

"Momma, is he going to live," cried a small female voice.

"Is Pilgrim coming back to us?" asked another in a waif like tone.

"Everyone move away. Don't crowd the man for goodness sake," said the first voice.

Pall felt himself in the arms of a man and woman. One of them wiped his mouth with a wet cloth. Another wiped his head.

"He's bleeding here, Tom," she said.

"Yes, Alicia, I know. Thank you."

"We've got to move him away from this wet ground," Alicia urged.

"We will. Be patient. First we got to get him up and across the ford. Kindly bring Alicia close so we can get him on her back.

The large draft horse was brought over next to where Pall was on the ground.

With the equipment and stores that were left on and around the canvas tarp, Tom built a crude series of steps. When he was done putting it together, he had his wife bring Alicia over to the other side of the steps.

"Hold her still, dear one, please," he asked.

Pall found, with Tom's help—for the young man knew now where he was in time—that he could stand and help Tom assist him up the makeshift stairs and onto the horse.

Once on, Tom got on in back of him.

His wife handed him the reins.

"Please get on the other horse, Alicia, and help me ride with me across the ford."

They successfully brought Pall across the ford to the far side of the road. Tom and Alicia took him off the horse. Tom carried him over and laid him down on a blanket that Alicia had just previously placed in the emerging green grass on the side of the wagon road.

Alicia brought some water over to him. Tom took it and again asked, "Are you all right, Pall?"

"Yes," he somewhat managed to say.

"We thought we lost you, Pilgrim," Alicia said with worry.

Tom observed that Pall's eyes were beginning to focus on things around him. "Please try to drink some water. You've earned it," he said.

"Da, Ma, is he alive?!" shouted Mary and Myra together from the other side of the washout.

"Yes, girls, he's coming back to us," Tom shouted back to them. "Be patient, your ma is coming over to get you."

Alicia nodded and went to get her daughters.

After she had gone to get them, Tom asked again, "Are you going to be okay, Pall?"

"Yes," came a firmer answer.

"From where I stood, I didn't think you were going to get hit by that rope. You responded quick to its breaking in half. Had you not moved when you did, I'm sure you wouldn't be talking with me now."

"I'll be okay, Tom: but I'm pretty shaken up. It felt like I was in a siege and near a loaded ballista when the rope had been cut in half."

"Are you sure you're alright?" Tom asked him again with added concern. He noticed a sheen of perspiration on the young warrior's forehead. Pall's eyes had gone out of focus again, too.

"Yes, Tom, I'll be fine."

Tom left Pall's side and went over to check on Alicia the horse, who nuzzled him back when he began rubbing her nose.

"We were lucky!" he said to his wife as she returned on Tom the horse. Mary was riding in front. Myra was holding onto her back.

"Yes, Tom," she responded. "But we were blessed more."

"Aye, Lass," he agreed softly.

"Where are my girls!" Tom hollered more than asked.

They came spilling over one another to him. He gave them hugs and rubbed the tops of their heads.

"Thank you for your prayers. We couldn't have done it without you saying them."

After hugging their father, Mary and Myra ran over to Pall. "You okay, Pilgrim with a double L?" they laughed.

"Yes, girls, I'm fine. Thank you for caring about me."

The girls went silent. They looked at their mother. Both of the little ones started crying.

"It's okay; everyone's fine," she reassured them.

"We could have lost someone," Myra said.

"Or, lost Alicia the horse," contributed Mary.

"Yes, we could have had something bad happen. But we're all safe," Tom said, trying to distract them from their morbid thoughts. "Come now, let's gather the rest of our belongings and get them across to where the wagon is waiting for us to continue on our journey. We've taken too much time being here."

That statement being made, they eventually accomplished that very task.

CHAPTER NINETEEN

They had travelled for about two hours since they left the area of the flooded road. The forest that had been around them relinquished its hold on the road and retreated back to the extent that they were passing through more open stretches, glades, meadows and sometimes open land itself.

Another hour passed and Tom decided to spell the horses, as well as themselves, for a brief while.

Pall had ridden in the back of the wagon where Alicia and Tom made a space for him. For some reason, he felt that he should not go to sleep. He had asked if the twins could ride in the back of the wagon with him. Alicia agreed that it was not a good idea to go to sleep immediately after being hit in the head as dramatically as he had beside the ford.

Mary and Myra kept up a constant round of conversation. If they weren't talking with Pall, they were commenting about what they were seeing as the wagon moved down the road, or they talked with one another.

Alicia impressed upon them the importance of their being back in the wagon with the young man. "Keep him talking if you can," she told them.

"Why, Ma," asked Mary.

"Because he could get worse after he was hurt so badly. And if that happens, going to sleep is not a good thing."

"What bad thing could happen to Pilgrim?" Myra asked her mother.

Ignoring the substance of the question, Alicia instead skirted the answer saying, "He needs to stay awake so we can watch how well he is doing. If he falls asleep we won't know that."

"Oh," both girls said.

With big smiles on everyone's face, the girls proudly rode in the back with Pall. They were very caring and solicitous toward him, at first. After a while, however, their attention turned to the stories their parents traditionally would tell them at night before they went to sleep.

An argument broke out between them. It became quite heated in its intensity, so much so that it roused Pall from almost falling asleep.

"Here, here," he said trying to calm them down. "What are you two fighting over?" he asked them.

"We were talking about the barrels Da made and if they could float with people in them," Mary informed him.

"I said that they could float people in them," Myra shared with Pall.

"I said that they couldn't take any more than one small person," Mary added.

"I said that they were strong barrels like the ones Da makes," Myra said.

"I said that those barrels could take more than one small person," Mary countered.

"Well even if they could, they still wouldn't fit more than one small person," insisted Myra.

"Yes, they could."

"No, they could not."

"Yes...."

"Okay, okay stop for a moment," Pall pleaded with them. "Why is this matter so important?" Pall asked the two of them.

Mary patiently explained the reason to Pall. Myra added important details.

"All of us are on a journey," Mary admitted to Pall solemnly.

"Yes, just like in almost all of the stories we're told," contributed Myra.

"One time there were thirteen dwarves..." Mary started to explain.

"And an old burglar, too," Myra interjected.

"Myra, stop talking! I'm the one telling Pilgrim what's going on."

"It's all right, girls," Pall said soothingly, "You can both tell me. Just be patient with one another."

Pall watched the frowns disappear, and smiles replace them.

"Well, Da said that the burglar helped his friends each get in a barrel," said Mary.

"Yes," Myra agreed, "and he put them into a stream like the one we had to cross this morning."

"And they escaped from the supspecious elves," Mary said with finality.

"Suspecial," Myra said in a singsong voice.

The girls started to argue over which was the proper way of saying the word.

"Wait, now, wait," Pall gently admonished them. "The word is suspicious. Do you know what it means?" he asked them.

"No," they both answered.

"Suspicious means that the elves didn't trust the others. They thought they had done something wrong," Pall explained.

At that moment the wagon came to a stop. Tom and Alicia decided to check on their passengers.

"Yes, but," Mary said, "they escaped from the elves in a stream like the one we had to cross."

"We should have done the same thing," Myra said.

"Yes, and that way you wouldn't have gotten hurt, Pilgrim," Mary concluded with tears in her eyes.

Pall did not quite know what to say to all of that.

Tom, however, had reached the back of the wagon and, based on what discussion he had heard between them, offered to resolve it for them.

"You are both very good listeners to the stories your mother and I share with you," he said.

All three of them in the wagon looked at Tom with wide open eyes.

"You're both right about this story. The barrels could float us down the current. And it is nice for me to see how kind you are about our friend Pall. But then, what would we do with our beautiful horses, Tom and Alisha?

"Oh," all three of them answered.

Alicia had arrived toward the end of the discussion. When she heard Tom's explanation and his audience's unanimous, single word response, she broke out in a fit of laughter.

"What's so funny?" all four of them asked her.

No answer was given.

Alicia went into a gale of laughter at that point in time.

Tom, acting upon Alicia's suggestion, had brought the wagon to a stop. He made sure the reins were tied off properly, and the brake was securely set.

The horses shook themselves, glad to have a rest at last.

"Look," Tom said in admiration, "a Sentinel Tree all alone in that glade."

A hundred feet off the road stood a magnificent looking copper beech.

While the light of the sun shone luminously, the tree itself also sent out a light of its own.

239

"There's a light shining from the tree itself," Alicia wondered out loud to Tom.

"I think it's one of God's candles," said Tom.

They held one another's left and right hands together.

Quiet reigned. The husband and wife could hear the girls in the back of the wagon talking and laughing together with Pall.

"It is a wonder of beauty," Alisha said after a while.

"Let's show our fellow travelers, too," said Tom.

They walked to the back of the wagon. Tom put down the tailgate.

"Do you all want to see one of the Lord's candles burning?" Alicia asked.

The girls ran to their mother, who took them in her arms. She brought them over to the middle of the wagon so they could view the whole scene.

"What do you say, Pall? You ready to take a look as well?" Tom asked.

"It's a lone Sentinel Tree?" Pall asked back to Tom.

"Yes. The sight is uncommon. It looks like a piece of the Garden."

Pall's eyes took on an eager light of interest. He moved toward Tom who helped give him a shoulder off the wagon.

Both walked to where Alicia and the twins stood looking in respect and love at the tree.

"Can we go there?" they asked her eagerly.

Tom and Alicia looked at one another to see what the other was thinking. They turned to look at Pall.

"Would you like to get closer, too?" Alicia inquired of him.

"Yes. Can we take the wagon underneath it and rest a bit there?"

"Let's check the lay of the field and see if we can take a loaded wagon on it securely," Tom answered.

Tom first entered the glade and told Pall what to look for in making sure the ground was solid and level enough to take a team of horses and wagon across its terrain.

They came to a gradual stop when they reached the edge of the Sentinel's canopy.

"There must be some kind of heat running out of this lord of the forest," Tom said.

"Yes," Pall said in agreement with Tom's observation. "Except we can't see it with the eyes we have."

"Well, Pilgrim," Tom said. "I can see the air move around its leaves, bark and trunk like I can when I watch the fire in a smith's forge."

Not commenting directly about the tree's power, Pall suggested to Tom, "If we rest here, I think we should put the wagon on the outside of its crown of leaves."

241

They walked back to Tom's family and all the property they had together.

Tom turned to Pall as they continued walking back to the wagon. "Who's Evangel?" He asked Pall with great interest.

Tom's question seemed to make the young warrior's ears ring. Pall felt slightly dizzy. *Not again!* he said to himself.

Pall opened his eyes and saw that Tom was helping hold him from falling to the soft, long grass underfoot.

We've stopped walking, Pall thought blearily.

"Must be the heat coming off the tree," he said aloud to Tom.

Tom looked in concern at his newfound ally.

"Pray give me but a moment, and I will be back to my old humor, friend Tom," Pall requested.

Alicia had walked out to them seeing Pall's distress.

The couple walked on either side of Pall, ready to help him stand if he required such aid.

Alicia and Tom helped guide him to the back of the wagon.

The twins expressed dismay at Pall's setback.

Before he climbed back into the wagon, he gently placed his hands on their heads. "Thank you for your care," he said softly to them.

"Thank you for your mercy to a fallen pilgrim," he said to husband and wife.

The adults helped him get up over the edge of the gate.

Pall rested his head on his arms after he sank down on the wagon's floor.

He drifted into a fog. Nothing happened to him there, at first. He thought he had gotten up and walked into the light of the old Sentinel in the glade before them. He curled up into a ball at the base of the tree and fell into a deep healing sleep.

It was late afternoon when he awoke from his rest. To his surprise, Pall saw that he was in the wagon and not stretched out on the ground beneath the Sentinel. He half expected to hear the creak and feel the sway of the wagon moving on the road. However, no sound or movement from it was felt. He easily got up and climbed down from its bed.

The sun was low in the western horizon. The heat from the day was cooling off.

He looked at the Sentinel.

The light being emitted from it seemed even more in evidence than before his rest and despite being in the full light of the setting sun.

Alicia said to him while he gazed at the tree, "We decided to stay here for the evening."

Pall nodded with relief at hearing this news.

"We all can use the rest," Tom said.

"Look, Pilgrim," Mary said, "we made camp right near this beautiful tree."

Surprisingly, Myra had nothing to share aloud. She took Pall by his left hand, instead.

They had a light and early supper. Having a fire was not even considered, especially in the presence of the Sentinel.

Their camp already had been made. Night came swiftly.

The tree lit the area in saffron, crimson and copper hues. The flames coming off it were now quite palpable, shimmering in a vision of beauty rarely seen in this life.

Mesmerized by the tree's overall countenance, Pall fell into a daze. He found that he could not fall asleep. He was agitated about something he could not fully express to himself.

Everything was quiet, except for the slight sound of the tree's leaves moving in rhythm with its glow.

He could feel the light of the tree beating gently against his half–closed eyes.

The young man sighed. His eyes fluttered closed.

In the meadow, on the other side of the wagon away from the Sentinel Tree, the air was disturbed.

Something in a tremor of its own light was breaking into shape.

It glistened; appeared. Vanished.

Rapidly winking into being seen and not seen many times over, had any human present but looked at it, the creature finally materialized into a solid shape of horror. It remained silent.

Neither the song of a wood thrush nor the hum of a cricket sounded.

Ünger had learned to keep its mouth shut.

"Arise, o man of dust. A great danger betides you and yours. It looms wide from the maw of hell."

Pall's eyes opened. With full awareness, he knew what was occurring.

He grabbed his scabbarded falchion. As he leaped to the ground off the wagon gate, he drew his sword.

In the light of the copper beech's flame, the blade stood in full view.

Ünger was ten feet away from the wagon, flashing in and out of view in quick succession.

It was in the form of a standing serpent. Its tongue flicked hungrily.

Pall addressed it formally:

"You have a fatal error made.
Rampage or not, you are a shade
of the foulest kind—made in secret.
Thou art but denied the banquet
with the just; inside the circle
of this guardian, you are anvil
to the God who'll hammer onto
you the perfumed fruit of death's slue."

Pall heard a clicking sound tick lightly out of Ünger's throat. It spoke in rough phrasing to him, as if unused to speech.

"Immortal you may think you be
in this false light shat by this tree.
Neither sword nor lord will deter
My master's will or my hunger.
You may foolishly choose to fight
me; your splinter has not the might
to vanquish the likes of my spirit.
Your false challenge has no merit."

Tom appeared on Pall's left side, carrying Myra in his arms.

Alicia approached Pall on his right, holding Mary in hers.

Ünger approached to within five feet of the humans. It growled at them in a guttural smacking sound. Drool from its mouth dripped onto the ground in streamlets of steam.

Pall softly said to his friends, "We need to move underneath the tree's leaves."

Ünger chuckled deeply from its throat.

"I will move behind you to my left. You move to your right. Get behind the wagon into the tree's protection."

"Nay, human flea," Ünger continued addressing Pall formally, "you are not manifest with the power to prohibit my probity."

Pall started to move to his left.

Alicia and Tom moved to their right.

The demon creature burbled, chirped and spat more fluid out of its mouth.

Just as each of the humans started to take their respective turn around the front and back ends of the wagon, the beast flared into its lizard shape.

Its tongue flickered forth a reddish orange flame that spewed out into a sickly green, condensed fire. It was hurled directly at Tom.

The cooper dodged quickly away from the foul discharge, unharmed.

All of them managed to reach their respective final turn to the other side of the wagon.

Ünger showed a great distaste of the tree's light. With a yowl of aggrieved frustration it translated itself before the right side of the wagon. It had interposed its body between the tree and Alicia.

247

It knew that these two females were the weakest and the most precious to the men.

On the other side of the wagon, Pall saw the demon's pernicious move against Alicia and Mary. He shouted at Ünger.

The monster uttered its weird laugh once more. Ünger ejected another gush of green fire.

The gleam of the beast's discharge overwhelmed mother and daughter. Devoured by its corruption, they disappeared from sight.

The sword in Pall's hand became enflamed from the light it had been absorbing from the tree. It burst forth into a shock of flame. Copper, crimson, gold, and carmine colors exploded into a consuming fire.

The young warrior flung it at the creature gloating at him in triumph.

It hit the lizard squarely in its center.

It laughed once more victoriously. It puffed itself up in pride.

The eruption from Pall's sword enveloped the monster.

It laughed again. It swaggered in sheer delight of its supremacy.

From inside himself, Pall brought forth more energy into the sword. He shouted the word, "Ruin!"

A scream of pure anguish poured out of the creature.

The young warrior, infused with the heat of battle, sheathed his sword and charged the demon at the same time.

Tom screamed his anger and dismay at both combatants.

Pall reached the lizard. He grabbed it by the tongue and snout and hurled it further towards the center of the Sentinel Tree.

The light of the tree burned its way into the lizard, going far deeper than Pall's sword had been able to do.

Ünger exploded in a way like the rope had in Pall's hands when it snapped in half. Pieces pouring off the creature's three forms seared away from the center of its flickering body, singeing and singing their way in every direction.

Bits of what remained of Ünger continued sliding off its body, alighting on the ground in desultory fashion.

Tom, Myra and Pall could not hear anything. They had become deaf with the destruction of the demon before them.

Both men fell on their knees to the ground, stunned into disbelief.

The sound of Myra's keening lapped onto the tree's burning light.

End of *THE PENITENT – PART I*

CAST OF CHARACTERS

PROLOGUE

Professor Melvin Tobin, Ph.D. (2065–2189): A former internationally known and respected professor. Upon retiring, he was unanimously granted the status of emeritus professor by his peers at Harvard University in Cambridge, Massachusetts on Old Earth. During his research and teaching years at Harvard, Professor Tobin held three endowed chairs in Philosophical Systems, Intelligence Engineering and Quantum Genetics. He was a specialist in evolutionary intervention.

PART ONE

Aldric: A warrior at the great convocation of Western Isles forces held on the headland overlooking Ringing Bay.

Sergeant Burchard: A veteran soldier of the elite Aeonian Guard, serving in the Northern Army of Ranulf Ealhhere, King of West Fündländ.

Carac (also known as **"First"** or **"Twin"**): A member of **Commander Gregor Mordant's Marauders**. He and Merek are identical twins.

Tom & Alicia Cooper: A married couple who are the parents of fraternal twins, **Mary** & **Myra Cooper**. Tom has been hired by the Town of Gullswater to be its new cooper.

Demesne of the Copper Beeches (also known as the **"Demesne of the Sentinels"**): These trees stand as Sentinels of the northern forest. A few humans know them **as** the Wood of the Royal Guard. They are sentient, puissant and mighty beings protecting this part of the world.

Error: Captain of Commander Gregor Mordant's Marauders.

Evangel: A young woman with a powerful presence and charismatic personality whom Pall seems to meet in a vision. In a soldier's uniform that is eerily similar to the one Pall wears, she addresses the military convocation of the Western Isles forces. Upon seeing one another, they sense that an immediate and surprisingly powerful bond is established between them.

Greatworth: An elderly man who is a hermit. He is one of the central figures Pall notices at the military convocation that takes place on the promontory overlooking Ringing Bay. Greatworth is accompanied by three silver-grey, great wolves.

Herald: A messenger of the **Risen One**.

Captain Joseph Martains: A captain of the elite Aeonian Guard who serves as an adjutant to **High Marshall Solace Umbré**. Both men serve in the Northern Army of **Ranulf Ealhhere**, King of West Fündländ.

Sergeant Meginhard: A veteran soldier of the elite **Aeonian Guard**, serving in the Northern Army of Ranulf Ealhhere, King of West Fündländ.

Merek (also known as "**Second**" or "**Twin**"): A member of Commander Gregor Mordant's Marauders. He and Carac are identical twins.

Commander Gregor Mordant: The leader of Mordant's Marauders, he officially serves as a key member of King Ranulf Ealhhere's intelligence service.

Mustard (also known as "Gordo" or Gordon): A member of Commander Gregor Mordant's Marauders.

The Nine Companions | Recruits: First joined together intoa regular unit of the Northern Army of

Ranulf Ealhhere, King of West Fündländ. They underwent a battle to the death to be accepted into the elite Aeonian Guard.

1. Jarin de Ashton
2. Ector Collier
3. Thurstan Gage
4. Brom Hovey
5. Samar Jackson
6. Adam Underhill
7. William Victor
8. Pall Warren
9. Rulf the Younger

The Rover Captain: A slightly built, white-haired ancient, Pall notices him driving a wagon drawn by a single black stallion in the center of the military convocation where he meets Evangel. The Captain is accompanied by 15 of his men. He is rumored to have been touched by Others.

John Savage (also known as "**the bowman**" or "**the archer**") **:** Plays a major leadership role in **King Ranulf Ealhhere's** intelligence.

Savaric (also known as "**the giant**"): A veteran soldier of the elite Aeonian Guard, serving in the Northern Army of Ranulf Ealhhere, King of West Fündländ.

High Marshall Solace Umbré: The leader of the elite Aeonian Guard, serving in the Northern Army of Ranulf Ealhhere, King of West Fündländ.

Ünger: A name of a class of demons, individually and collectively. It has the capacity to divide itself into three separate creatures in the respective shapes of a snake, a lizard and a panther.

The Ünger is completely inimical to human beings. It can be difficult to see because of its peculiar qualities in moving from place to place, as well as its shape shifting features in going from transparent, blurred to opaque states of being.

It is almost impossible to kill. It destroys human beings by eviscerating and consuming all of the internal parts of the body, leaving the external skin and hair intact.

Valravn: John Savage best describes this powerful entity. "A Valravn is a supernatural bird. Its name means raven of the slain. Eating the heart of a king on a field of battle as it told us, means that it's become a terrible animal."

David & Lucia Warren: Pall Warren's biological father and stepmother. Formerly the High Commander of King Ranulf Ealhhere's Northern Armies, he retired early to become a master blacksmith in a small village in West Fündländ.

Pall Warren: Raised in a small village in West Fündländ by David and Lucia Warren, Pall becomes one of the finest young warriors of his time. He is especially gifted in hand–to–hand combat with the quarterstaff, falchion sword and fighting knives. He has been deeply touched by the Hand of God.

Post a Review

If you liked reading *THE PENITENT – PART II,*
please post a review at immortalitywars@gmail.com.

EXCERPT FROM
THE PENITENT – PART II

CHAPTER ONE

She had been in this small house in the woods ever since she could remember being there. It was home to her, even though it was not her first one. Everything in it was comfortable and put in the right places.

She did not live with her parents. She had been adopted informally by Matthew Greatworth. Matthew called himself a hermit. However, folks who lived nearby considered him merely a recluse. In any event, hermit, recluse, both, or none at all, Matthew withdrew himself from the company of humans because he felt distracted by them. Alone, without the ongoing trauma and drama of living amongst mortals, Matthew could seek the living presence of God.

He was free from the daily chores of social and community obligations. When he felt the hand of God upon him, he could investigate, pray and discern this touch of the divine will with as much concentration as he cared to expend on it. No one bothered him. He bothered no one at all. Matthew would sometimes characterize these two former statements as having great worth.

"And, that's why the good God gave me my name," he would chuckle.

While he was very practical, he was also very absent minded, particularly when he was communing in the spirit.

It was Matthew who found her.

She had been but a baby abandoned by fate, human cruelty, and/or the lord of sin on a rural road. Greatworth would argue with himself over this very issue for many years. Her parents were lying dead in the middle of the lane. Their throats were cut. Their bodies were violated. There was no mercy to be had in this scene. Except for the fact that an intuition of danger crossed her mother's awareness before she and her husband were so senselessly murdered, Jacquelyn Blessingvale would never be thinking the thoughts pouring out of her memories even now. She would have been dead.

That day of prophetic mercy saw one of the many roving bands of outlaws raiding the Blessingvale caravan.

Her mother's intuition and foresight spared her baby's life. Before these brigands brutalized the Blessingvales, she had run unobserved off the road. She carried her child to a ditch and placed her in the bottom. A thicket of alders next to it helped camouflage the spot even more. The baby was swaddled securely and covered with a blanket.

A day later after this fatal tragedy occurred, Matthew was in one of his distracted phases. He was not paying attention to where he was walking. As a matter of fact, he was off to the side of the road, strolling along in a roughly parallel position with it. He was arguing with himself over some arcane matter concerning the nature of a miracle.

The laws of nature are suspended when a miracle occurs, was one of the strands of argument he was considering.

"Although," he countered aloud to no one in particular, "the very fact that a miracle occurs may mean that the laws of nature aren't suspended, but fulfilled instead."

Well, if that is true, miracles should be occurring all of the time, but they don't.

"Matthew, just because one cannot see such with the eyes of man, does not mean that miracles are not occurring."

True, true, but this is mere confusion. When a blind man's sight is healed with the touch of a prophet, the laws of sickness, maladies and death are set aside. If these axioms were not set aside there would be no miracle.

"Look here, a miracle happens because the presence of God is the realization of natural and spiritual law. Every moment in time is filled with this potential. We have but to invoke it in faith for it to be seen in our presence. It's like falling..."

With the last word uttered, Matthew, not looking at all where he was going, fell into a ditch. When he hit the bottom of it, he completed his proposition saying, "...into a ditch."

Finding himself lying on his back at the bottom, he stared uncomprehendingly at the sky above him. Gaining his wits about him, he railed at himself internally, *What kind of miracle is this now?*

Matthew stood up and shook the dirt and dust off him. He looked to see if he was still hale. He checked for cuts, bruises or sprains.

Seeing that he was fine he said, "No broken bones: looks like a minor miracle just occurred."

The hermit moved to his right to get a better purchase onto the ground so he could work his way out of the hole into which he had fallen. He felt his foot hit something soft.

Paying no attention to it, he concentrated on getting out of the ditch.

He reached the top and started walking away.

He thought he mistakenly heard the faint snuffle and low gurgling of a baby.

Of late, he had been hearing many odd noises. He passed it off as an internal clangor and mental noise that comes with being an older person.

"Perhaps these sounds I am hearing are just a result of my infernal caterwauling to myself," he said with a distracted and impatient air.

I am just going to let two auditory hallucinations of a baby rattle away somewhere else, he added internally with growing irritation.

Assured with the fact that he had solved this annoyance to his satisfaction, Greatworth continued walking. "Thank the good Lord; I'm out of that trap to the unwary."

Mere misapprehension, Matthew snorted derisively. *I may as well think I heard a troll tell me a new perspective on the origins of life where I fell.*

"It could well be an angel," he countered.

Or, a very clever troll, came his immediate response.

Behind him, a baby's laughing and cooing resounded from the side of the road into which he had tumbled.

He ceased arguing with himself. The hermit was now curious to discover the true origin of the sounds he thought he just heard. He took them as a sign to go back over to the ditch and investigate further. Greatworth used the baby's voice as an aural beacon to guide himself by to help find her. Soon enough, he discovered her lying near the bottom of the ditch from which he had just extracted himself.

Picking her up carefully, and cooing at her as he carried her back up the ditch, he reached level ground. Matthew sat down on the side of the road with her still in his arms.

After a while, the misshapen bodies, broken and pillaged cart in the center of the road, and scattered and ripped clothes of the miserable tableau before him, attracted his attention. He got up onto his feet and looked around at an appalling scene of pillage and rapine.

Upon looking closer at the details of this crime, he found a leather pouch thrown carelessly on top of a small opened case. He set both aside for his purposes of rescuing her from this place. With one hand holding the baby, he used the other to gather together the baby's clothing into the case. Any papers that he also found were put into the leather pouch. There were no valuables, coins or jewelry, in evidence.

He completed his task of collecting the items he thought a baby would need.

Looking over all of the carnage committed there, while keeping the babe in his gentle but firm grasp, he prayed over the dead.

When he was finished praying, he looked at the baby again. She looked back at him with a steadiness and intelligence that melted his old heart.

"How did you survive this attack, little one?" he gently asked her.

Someone, her mother or father, must have put her in the trench for safekeeping, he considered silently.

"These bodies have been here awhile: at least a day. It's a miracle she's survived this violence, and another one as well that she's not dead from starvation, thirst or the further depredation of humans and wild animals."

Looks like we have found an angel after all, he wryly said to himself. *There is goodness and innocence in the world if we but look for it.*

"Yes," he agreed. Good news has always been told by the angels of the Lord."

I think we should name her, he said silently..." Evangel," he completed aloud.

CHAPTER TWO

Matthew had taken her to his home in the forest. He called the forest God's Temple. The home he lived in was called The Refuge.

When the weather was warm, both of them would bring into their household flowers, leaves and anything interesting that they could easily carry with them. These daily trophies of nature's beauty were used to great effect in decorating the small home.

"It isn't much," she frequently said aloud to the house, "but it's perfect, nevertheless."

The Refuge had a common room, which Matthew whimsically called a great room. In this room was a fireplace that served the purposes of providing heat, light and a place to cook food. A medium sized, oaken table, hand built by him, sat near a window where they ate their meals. There was a pantry area for storing seasonings, spices and herbs, as well as for holding utensils used for cooking and eating. A small, compact room was employed as a library and devotional for Matthew. Matthew slept in the bedroom on the first floor. Evangel used the loft for her sleeping quarters. A small basement underneath the floor of the great room was used to store wine, vegetables, dried meat, butter, milk, cheese and other victuals.

Long ago, when Matthew first found this spot, he built a temporary structure to live in nearby while he built his home. When he was finished constructing it, he knocked down the makeshift quarters and put in its place a hidden safe room underneath the ground. He never had to use it, but he believed in providing contingencies against any random events, and purposeful attacks, from hell, or from human beings, and even bad weather, for that matter.

A case in point is what happened to Evangel's parents, he would sometimes emphasize to himself.

Matthew never seemed at a loss to help her adjust to the different phases of her growing up. He would tell her in his own unique way what life was offering or denying her. And she understood what he was trying to say to her.

Despite his care, and probably because of it, in making sure that she had a picture in her mind of her parents and who they were to her, she loved Matthew as the grandfather the Good Lord gave her on this worldly plane.

As she became older and the issues of life became more complex, Matthew was able to explain to her in a more mature way the complexity about what was happening inside her. If he could not help her, he would find a way to do so. For example, when she first became a woman he brought one of the nuns from the not too distant St. Åyrwyus Priory to stay with them for a month. Her name was Murial. The two women became close friends with one another.

In taking care of her, Matthew was always careful to tell her who her parents were. Even though he had never met them, he knew enough about them from what he could glean from other people who had known them. He had also read a diary that both her father and mother kept. He thought it important that their memory be kept sacred and honored for her.

Matthew told her early on in Evangel's life that her surname was Blessingvale. "Your first name was Jacquelyn."

"Isn't that my name still?" she would ask him.

"Yes, child," he responded. "But the name God gave you through me is Evangel."

"Can I still keep my last name, Grandfather?"

Matthew nodded distractedly at her as he was already becoming lost in an internal argument with himself over the corruption of holy vows in the Church.

"Evangel Blessingvale," she pronounced slowly and with pride. "Sounds like a holy prophet, doesn't it, Grandfather?"

"Mmmmmnnn, more like prophetess, lass."

"Does a prophetess get to talk with God almost every day, too?" She first asked him this question when she was very young. It was often one—as was the topic of this conversation—that became almost a ritual of discussion between them.

Her comment helped bring Greatworth back to paying attention to her. "I think that goes with the crops in the fields, as with the trees in the forest, and the fish in the sea, little one."

"You always answer me with funny words."

"Yes, Evangel," he replied with a slight hint of exasperation. "A prophetess is a girl, or a woman, who does talk with God almost every day. Please forgive my inattention."

"It's okay, Grandfather, I know you're trying to talk with yourself about something important."

Matthew smiled at the generosity of spirit she always showed him.

He was never mad with her. While she was a child who was full of life, energy and the restlessness of curiosity, he never had reason to become upset with her over bad behavior. A part of him wanted her to adopt his last name because she profoundly had become a great worth to him.

Evangel Greatworth sounds exactly right to me, he mused with certitude.

A thought tugged on him concerning what she had just asked him about being with God. "Does God talk with you?" he asked.

"No, Grandfather, I talk with him mostly."

"Mostly!" he said somewhat surprised.

She looked at him with her hazel green eyes and nodded her head in agreement.

"Does God answer you sometimes, child?" he asked with gentle and great interest.

Again, she looked at him and nodded her head.

"Do you hear His voice," he asked in awe.

"No," she answered right away. "He sometimes shows me things, though."

Greatworth now said nothing. He looked at the little girl before him with childlike simplicity of his own. He waited patiently for her to explain more about what she had just told him.

"He shows me in dreams, or in pictures. Sometimes a story comes to me and it's like you're reading it to me in a great book."

"What does the book look like?"

"It's on a table that's all alight. The book is in the middle of it. There are a lot of silver colored beings around in back of it. They're singing while holding spears in their hands."

Matthew blinked his eyes rapidly on hearing this information. "And, the book...."

"The book is hard to see because it keeps changing. The light pouring from it is brighter than the sun's."

"How do you know what's in it, dear one?"

"I hear your voice reading from it, Grandfather."

While Matthew had many other questions he wanted to ask her, he held off in doing so. She had just given him enough information for him to consider for a season and then some.

When she was eleven years of age, she went on a walk to one of her favorite places in the woods. It was a place that she had not visited for a while since the early spring. Thus, she was anxious to get there and see what nature had done in the meantime to it.

The pool of water with fish swimming in its depths was the same as it was the last time she was there. If anything, the depth of the water was a bit lower. The stream had not been replenished by the blessing of rain for almost a month.

The amount of water flowing over a series of waterfalls leading to it had significantly been lowered, too. The sound of it cascading over the rocks was not as loud as it had been when she was there last.

"Well, that simply makes it better for me to hear what else is happening here," she said audibly just to listen to the rhyme and the play on the same sounding words she made up on the spot.

She sat down near the pool's edge and leaned her head back against a young tree. The leaves in the oak tree above her rustled slowly in the gentle wind's caress. The stream pouring into the pool below her conversed with the leaves overhead in watery chattiness.

She fell asleep.

On the other side of the pool, deeper into the woods, a young wolf was giving birth to her first litter. It was struggling to stay alive in bringing her pups into the world.

Evangel could see this event happening in her dream.

She could sense there was something different about this animal. Several powers had settled on it. Three distinct entities had coalesced their might into its pain wracked body.

She felt no ill will in this triune force. She felt love, loyalty and a lethal desire to seek a wrong righted within it. She could not identify the source of this wrong.

Seven pups were delivered. Only three survived. They were very small. In truth, they were tiny. They were pure white. In the succession of their being birthed, one whined plaintively, the other gave a soft, husky sigh, while the third gasped, coughed and gulped for air desperately.

Arising from the dream, she unerringly went to the place where the mother wolf had given birth. When she arrived there, she found the wolf dead.

Tears fell from her eyes.

"Just like me," she said. "Born into the world with death all around you. No mother and father to protect you."

Don't be such a foolish goose, she thought to herself. *These are just animals.*

"They may be on the surface, but God showed me they are from his will."

She realized with a shock that she was talking to herself the way Matthew often did as well.

She became further surprised when she saw that she had come across a scene of tragedy just like her grandfather had so long ago when he found her in a ditch alongside the road.

"Well, there's nothing else to do but to take these three living ones home for Grandfather and I to take care of them."

What will you name them? she asked herself.

"Why that's simple. God's spirit already told me: Whimper, Whisper and Wheezer."

She carried them home with her.

When she told Matthew the story, he knelt down and hugged her. As tears fell from his eyes, he said, "Just like you said to yourself, you were brought to them by the Lord above to save and care for them. Like grandfather, like granddaughter."

Both laughed through their tears.

Matthew had Evangel bring him to the scene of the puppies' birth. He had brought a shovel with him. "We need to bury their mother and the other pups properly, and send them along with grace and mercy back to the Lord's domain."

With loving care all five animals were buried, and blessed as well with prayer and song.

They returned home soon afterwards.

When they arrived at the door to The Refuge, Evangel looked up at Matthew and said, "Does this mean that I am to be their grandmother, Matthew?"

Her use of his first name startled him. "No, child," he responded solemnly, "I would say that you are now a prophetess and protector to them."

Six years passed in the peace and in the prosperity of Matthew's profound care for her and for their three wards.

The time, on gossamer wings undaunted in its rush towards destiny, carried them in its swift current.

Life for these five was idyllic.

This sylvan span of life since Greatworth found her, stretching in length for almost a score of years, was shattered in her seventeenth.

End of *THE PENITENT – PART II,* **excerpt.**

ABOUT THE AUTHOR

A. Keith Carreiro earned his master's and doctoral degrees from Harvard Graduate School of Education, with the sequential help and guidance of three advisors, Dr. Vernon A. Howard, Dr. Donald W. Oliver and Professor Emeritus, Dr. Israel Scheffler. Keith's academic focus, including his ongoing research agenda, centers upon philosophically examining how creativity and critical thinking are acquired, learned, utilized and practiced in the performing arts. He has taken his findings and applied them to the professional development of educational practitioners and other creative artists.

Earlier in his teaching career he was a professor of educational foundations, teaching graduate students of education at universities in Vermont, Florida, Arizona, and Pennsylvania. He currently teaches as an adjunct professor of English at Bridgewater State University, as well as teaching English, philosophy, humanities and public speaking courses at Bristol Community College.

His research on creativity and critical thinking is based upon his experience in learning and performing on the classical guitar. He started studying this instrument at the age of four with Maestro Joseph

Raposo, Sr., and took lessons with him until the age of 17. Keith also studied music theory and composition with Maestro José da Costa of New Bedford, and classical guitar with Robert Paul "Bob" Sullivan of the New England Conservatory of Music.

In 1973 at Ithaca College, he attended a master class workshop conducted by Miguel Ablóniz of Milan, Italy. Ablóniz' knowledge about technique and aesthetics attained a worldwide influence about the nature of guitar practice and performance. Maestro Andrés Segovia considered Ablóniz to be one of the world's most esteemed classical guitar teachers.

During the 70s, Keith performed his music and selections from the classical guitar repertoire throughout North and South America. He had many opportunities to play with a wide variety of musicians, composers, singer/songwriters, choreographers, theater directors, performers and conductors.

Due to his love of family, he has seen his fervor for history, as well as his passion for wondering about the future, deepen dramatically.

He lives in Swansea, Massachusetts and has six children and 13 grandchildren. He belongs to an eighty-five-pound golden retriever and an impish Calico cat.

Made in the
USA
Middletown, DE